Shed in the City

De-ann Black

First published on Kindle 2014

Paperback edition published 2021

Shed in the City

ISBN: 9798513058809

Also by De-ann Black (Romance, Action/Thrillers & Children's books). See her Amazon Author page or website for further details about her books, screenplays, illustrations, art and fabric designs.
www.De-annBlack.com

Romance:

The Sewing Shop
Heather Park
The Tea Shop by the Sea
The Bookshop by the Seaside
The Sewing Bee
The Quilting Bee
Snow Bells Wedding
Snow Bells Christmas
Summer Sewing Bee
The Chocolatier's Cottage
Christmas Cake Chateau
The Beemaster's Cottage
The Sewing Bee By The Sea
The Flower Hunter's Cottage

The Christmas Knitting Bee
The Sewing Bee & Afternoon Tea
The Vintage Sewing & Knitting Bee
Shed In The City
The Bakery By The Seaside
Champagne Chic Lemonade Money
The Christmas Chocolatier
The Christmas Tea Shop & Bakery
The Vintage Tea Dress Shop In Summer
Oops! I'm The Paparazzi
The Bitch-Proof Suit

Action/Thrillers:

Love Him Forever.
Someone Worse.
Electric Shadows.

The Strife Of Riley.
Shadows Of Murder.

Children's books:

Faeriefied.
Secondhand Spooks.
Poison-Wynd.

Wormhole Wynd.
Science Fashion.
School For Aliens.

Colouring books:

Summer Garden. Spring Garden. Autumn Garden. Sea Dream.
Festive Christmas. Christmas Garden. Flower Bee. Wild Garden.
Faerie Garden Spring. Flower Hunter. Stargazer Space. Bee Garden.

Embroidery books:

Floral Nature Embroidery Designs
Scottish Garden Embroidery Designs

Contents

CHAPTER ONE

Tea Bread and a Garden Gnome

The large garden gnome was awkward to carry so I resorted to lifting him by the back of his trousers because I could slip my hand into the dent in his bum and lug him along by his arse handle.

I carried the gnome through the centre of Glasgow at 3:00am in the morning. The icy wind cut along the street and I shivered in the cold. My fingers were freezing.

It was the last week of January, frost glittered on the streets. I was wrapped up against the cold in a warm jacket, boots and a woolly hat.

I'd been unable to sleep for the excitement of owning my own tearoom and bakery serving traditional baking and teatime treats. And from the heartache that Jason had left me with nothing but the debt of the new venture and a bug–eyed gnome that resembled him in all sorts of uncanny ways.

He'd bought it because he liked it and said it looked like his grandfather. I thought it had skipped a couple of generations and looked like Jason when he was displeased with me. It was an expression I was familiar with, especially recently when we'd decided to open a tearoom in Glasgow. Not content with opening up something we'd never owned before, we set up home in the city centre, moving from Jason's lovely house on the outskirts of Glasgow into the tiny flat above the tearoom. I tried to talk Jason into being sensible. He was the sensible sort. I was the bad influence, or so he called me, quite often as I recall.

I had loved Jason, I'm sure I had. We had a comfortable relationship rather than one of those torrid romances where I'd rip his clothes off whenever we were in the bedroom. Jason complained if I tugged his shirt in the heat of passion in case he lost a button.

Wild nights with him were confined to breaking open a bottle of wine and falling asleep watching a film on television followed by a quick fumble and a roll in the duvet. I told myself that wild notions were transient and that one day I'd be glad that Jason was the buttoned up, dependable and trustworthy type. Unfortunately, he turned out to be a lying, cheating rotter who had been planning to ditch me for a while, but he'd never lost a button, not while I was dating him.

I was now responsible for making this venture work while Jason went to live with his brother in London. Jason was dating someone else. I'd suspected he'd been seeing her behind my back and that he'd been looking for a chance to leave me in Glasgow while he made a new life for himself in London. And I was right. All those late nights working at the hotel, supposedly learning more catering skills, were a lie. He'd been a chef for several years, though I was the one who could rustle up a batch of tea bread and fairy cakes better than him.

My passion for home baking had led me to working part–time from home, supplying birthday and celebration cakes. I'd taken courses in baking and cake decorating. Meanwhile, Jason had been too busy cheating on me with whatshername. No wonder his pastries were as useless and flaky as he was.

As for me...well, I was determined to show Jason and his snooty family and whoever else sided with him rather than the wild little brunette (as Jason and his acquaintances liked to call me) that I could make the new tearoom a success. I was brought up in Glasgow. I loved everything about it. Glasgow had a fantastic mix of shops and districts that ranged from modern to traditional. The rainy days when the Scotch mist cast the city's magnificent skyline into soft focus were a pleasure. I enjoyed getting up early to see the day spring into life whatever the season. I loved to go for walks in the parks and garden areas that were dotted throughout the city. And most of all I loved the idea of owning a tearoom and bakery in Glasgow and baking cakes, bread, biscuits, shortbread and scones.

The tearoom had previously been a small restaurant. The kitchen was ideal for my baking. The premises had a long front counter where I could display my cakes, and six tables, each seating four people. Customers could pop in to buy a cake as if it was a bakery shop, or sit down and enjoy a cuppa and cake or scone.

Jason had done a runner, but I'd decided to stay and fight for the business. Not that I had much choice. All the legal aspects had been sorted by Jason and his lawyers, basically dumping the whole responsibility of the venture on to my shoulders — bastards. I'd paid three months lease on the tearoom premises, which included the flat above it, so I had to make this work before the lease payments were due again. I had a few thousand pounds in the bank, money I'd earned from my home baking and sewing work, but apart from that, my back was against the wall.

I had a lot of work to do — which included ditching Jason's plastic lookalike. The tearoom had patio doors at the back that led on to a garden and that's where he'd put the gnome. The property had once been a house and garden, but over the years the city had swallowed up the houses and transformed them into shops and businesses. Most had lost their gardens but thankfully the tearoom's garden had survived. It was long and narrow and could be accessed via the patio or the pathway that ran along the side of the tearoom. A metal gate at the front of the premises was kept locked, by me, to prevent intruders wandering in off the street.

A ramshackle shed cast a forlorn shadow across the patch of lawn at the back of the tearoom. With it being January I didn't plan to tackle the garden until the spring when hopefully I could plant lettuce and spring onions, perhaps herbs, though I'd never tried those, and flowers. Deep down, I was quite a crafty type, not in a sneaky way, but in a sewing, painting, baking and making stuff way. I'd worked in shops, offices and even a gym, never really finding my niche, but always veering back to creative pursuits especially baking cakes and sugarcraft.

The shed was tiny and I wasn't sure if I could restore it. Apart from cobwebs and a broken lawnmower, the only useful thing it contained was an old bicycle. Whoever had owned the bike had looked after it well. The frame was intact and the chain only needed oiling to make it run smoothly. I used the pump to blow up the tyres which were rather flat. I scrubbed the basket on the front until it was clean and two shades lighter. The old paintwork was chipped so I gave it a coat of pink paint and planned to put it outside the tearoom's front window during the day. I thought it would create a vintage look to the frontage and attract attention from passers–by. I'd pinned a notice to the window — *Tearoom opening soon.*

I'd worked for a month reorganising the tearoom, giving it a vintage vibe that Jason wouldn't have approved of. There was little in my life that he approved of, so although I was genuinely broken–hearted at being dumped by a two–timing weasel like him, he'd probably done me a favour by leaving. Now I could do what I

3

wanted. And that included finding a suitable home for the plastic gnome. It was creeping me out. Every time I looked at its features it reminded me of Jason.

The fact that I'd been involved with a sour–faced, cheating sneak who looked somewhat gnome–like made me realise that my life needed a complete overhaul. Starting with the gnome. Begone plastic lookalike. But I didn't want to throw him in the rubbish bin. There could be consequences. People didn't just throw gnomes away. They gave them to other people who loved them. I had to find somewhere that he could be picked up by some passer–by who thought — oh, there's a gnome without a home. I'll have him.

That was the plan. In the bleak glow of the frosty night I doubted I'd thought it through properly. The story of my life.

'Can I help you with your garden gnome, Miss?'

The voice sounded pleasant but authoritative. I glanced round and there was a police officer studying me and my plastic buddy.

I tried to smile but my grin was as plastic as the gnome. Was I in trouble? I was usually in trouble. According to Jason anyway.

'I, eh...'

'Do you need assistance?' he offered.

'No, I'm...' *What? Trying to stash a gnome where someone can steal him? Off–loading a lookalike of my ex–boyfriend?*

'Are you taking him home?' he said.

'No, I was...' *trying to lose him.*

'Is there a problem with the gnome?'

Oh yes. Where should I start?

'Put the gnome down and give me details of what the problem is.'

I sat him down, and sighed. 'Well...it's complicated.'

'Cut to the relevant parts.'

'My boyfriend dumped me and left me with the financial burden of a business, a tearoom near here, and a garden gnome that kind of looks like him.'

'Your ex–boyfriend looked like a gnome?'

'He was taller. A lot taller and he didn't wear a bobble hat or anything, but his features, particularly his hair that we used to agree looked like corrugated iron, sort of reminds me of him.'

'So you don't want to be reminded of your ex–boyfriend, and you want rid of the gnome?'

4

'Yes, but I didn't want to throw him in a bin or anything like that. I wanted to put him where someone would pick him up.'

He nodded thoughtfully. 'There's a small recycling unit over there. Sit him beside that rather than dump him inside it or he'll be melted down and —'

'End up as plastic forks in my tearoom takeaway.'

He laughed and picked up the gnome. 'I'll take him over there for you. I'm Doyle.'

'That's very kind of you, Officer Doyle.' I eased my shoulders from the dead weight of carrying the garden ornament.

'He's big, for a gnome, isn't he?'

'Yes, I think he's quite old, made when things were sturdier and made to last.'

A doleful expression fell across Doyle's manly features. 'Nothing lasts these days. Nothing.'

I got the impression he wasn't just talking about garden ornaments. Had a relationship gone bad? I didn't like to pry.

Doyle I reckoned was in his early thirties and a fine looking man whose broad shoulders suited wearing a uniform. His hair was light brown from what I could see. He wore a hat that shaded his pale grey eyes, and could've been a poster boy for a fit looking copper. If only all policemen looked so luscious. My heart gave a little flutter, or maybe I was just tired.

'You look tired,' he commented as I trudged along beside him.

'I've been working for a month without much sleep to get the tearoom ready for business. I'm giving it a traditional look. I've been sewing chintz curtains and painting the dressers and drawers. The tearoom has a lot of dark wood which is lovely, but I'm giving some of the second–hand furniture I bought a lick of cream and pastel coloured paint. Giving it a distressed look, as if it's worn.' Rather like me. At thirty, some days I felt worn to the bone. 'I'm creating a vintage theme.'

'Old–fashioned?'

'Yes. I'll be serving afternoon teas and traditional cakes and baking.'

'On your own?'

'It's a small tearoom. Obviously the original plan was for the two of us to bake and work together. But I think I can manage on my own. I plan to bake everything early in the morning before opening.

Then I'll serve customers myself. I don't expect to be busy to begin with and if the business picks up I'll hire someone to help me.'

'Good luck with that.'

'Thank you.'

He dumped, sorry...he put the gnome down where someone would be tempted to take him home.

'Thank you for your help, officer.' I went to hurry away before I got myself into further trouble.

'What's the name of your tearoom?'

I didn't have a name for it. Jason wanted to call it Jason's tearoom or something equally selfish. 'No name yet.'

He smiled. 'I'll pop into the *no name yet* tearoom soon. I'm not much of a tea drinker though.'

'My menu includes coffee and hot chocolate. And cocoa.'

He smirked. He definitely smirked at the mention of cocoa.

'I'll drop by then.'

'Great.' I smiled and made another bid to scurry away.

'What's your name?' he called to me.

'Hazel.'

I hurried away before he had a chance to ask me anything else.

He hadn't asked me where the tearoom was located. It wasn't far and I knew he watched which direction I headed in, so I took a diversion up another street to put him off the scent. Though I supposed he could track me down easily enough. How many Hazels were opening a new tearoom in the centre of Glasgow and lurking in the streets on a freezing cold night with a garden gnome?

As I walked towards the tearoom a wave of excitement went through me. The old–fashioned lamp on the counter gave a warm glow to the premises. The large front window that I'd cleaned and polished until my arms ached sparkled in the wintry light. There was no name above the entrance, but I'd painted the word *Tearoom* on the canopy above the door using lettering stencils and antique–look gold paint.

I unlocked the door and went inside. It had retained the warmth from earlier. I'd been firing up the catering ovens which had been part of the old restaurant premises. They were perfect for baking and also helped to heat the premises.

The original fireplace was situated in the main tearoom area. The hearth was small but when lit gave off a terrific heat. The tiles around the fireplace had cleaned up well. One of the tiles was cracked but it didn't matter. The whole look of the place was imperfect and I hoped customers would feel at home.

An old handcrafted wooden hive that reminded me of a large doll's house sat in the garden so I'd painted bumblebees into the decor along with butterflies and flowers, especially tea roses and pansies. I planned to sell jars of rose petal jam and honey and included a range of all–time favourite preserves on the menu. Damson and plum were the colours of the napkins and cushion covers on the chairs. I'd made the cushion covers myself from linen remnants I bought in a fabric shop in Glasgow, and found napkins online to match. I hoped to put trailing flowers in the bicycle basket when the weather was warm and decorate the frontage with hanging baskets of blue lobelia.

I'd bought four second–hand but working sewing machines at an auction in Glasgow. A job lot for very little cost. Near the back of the tearoom I'd set up four tables and chairs along one wall, each with a sewing machine. The tables were another bargain lot, none of them matching, and I'd painted them cream and embellished them with tea roses and pansies, either painted on or decorated with decoupage — fancy paper and artwork stuck on to the table tops and then coated with a varnish–like protector.

My aim was to create a little sewing bee niche within the tearoom where customers could have tea and cake and then use a sewing machine, for up to an hour, making whatever project they were sewing. I pictured customers coming in, chatting, sewing, making quilts and clothes. And I planned to use the sewing machines. Sewing was relaxing. I loved working with fabrics and thought that it would lend itself to the vintage theme of the tearoom. Jason would never have approved. He'd talked about having computers, like a cyber cafe, set up. I'd gone for the other end of the scale — sewing machines that I hoped customers would love as much as I did.

I flicked the lights off and headed upstairs.

A staircase led up to a small flat. Now that Jason had moved out it had more than enough space for me and my things. My bedroom at the back overlooked the garden and the ramshackle shed. I'd added little solar lights so the garden always had a glow to it at night. I pictured it would look lovely with a few flowers, a vegetable patch

7

and the postage stamp–size lawn tidied up. Though I wasn't sure what to do about the dilapidated shed.

The bathroom in the flat had a corner bath squeezed in with an overhead shower. The living room had rugs rather than carpeting, and I'd added throws and cushions to the sofa. I'd decorated the flat as I had the tearoom, to save money, refurbishing tattered chairs and items that were worn and frayed. I painted the chests of drawers in the living room and the wardrobe in the bedroom. I'd aired everything. We'd moved in when the weather was milder and I'd been able to keep the windows open to freshen the entire premises. Now that it was freezing, I liked snuggling on the sofa in front of the fire.

Wearing thermal jim–jams and fluffy socks, I climbed into bed. A bright moon shone in the clear dark sky and cast a glow across the room.

I thought about the garden gnome and wondered if anyone had stolen him yet.

CHAPTER TWO

Bumblebees and the Beemaster

Everything was ready for opening up the tearoom, except me. I'd planned to be so organised. Cakes, scones and bread baked. Display counter stocked. Fire lit to make the tearoom cosy and inviting on a frosty morning. Hair done, makeup on, flowery apron.

Jason's words reminded me of my shortfalls. '*You could create chaos in an empty house, Hazel.*'

At the time I'd argued that this was rubbish. I was efficient. However, having created bedlam in the kitchen trying to bake too many scones while icing cakes and running out of coal for the fire, I grudgingly saw Jason's point.

But I'd sorted out the baking. And I'd sprinted to the grocery shop nearby for a small bag of fuel for the fire. So everything in the tearoom was ready to roll, except me. My hair looked like I'd been through a wind tunnel. In a way I had, having dashed along the street on a frosty morning. My straight, shoulder–length brown hair usually behaves quite well. But not today. Typical.

I saw my face in the kitchen mirror. I looked so pale. I flicked on some mascara to emphasise my green eyes. My lipstick gave a soft sheen but there was no time to fuss with makeup. A customer was peering in the window. I put on a clean apron and tried to look efficient. I didn't stare at him. I arranged a tray of fruit scones and kept busy. The heat from the fire was starting to bring some warmth to my pale complexion. Or perhaps it was sheer harassment.

I sneaked a peek at him. Around six–foot–three, early thirties, lean but strong. His unruly dark blond hair blew about in the cold early morning wind and he pushed it back from his eyes so that he could read the menu that I'd pinned up. My heart gave an unexpected flutter, reacting nervously that he could be my first official customer or that he was sexy as hell.

The bell on the door tinkled as he came in.

He wore a cream cotton shirt, a heavy cotton, collarless with the top button undone that made my wicked imagination picture him getting ready for bed. Or perhaps he was just up. A morning person, like me, although I was also a night owl. His wore a long, dark greatcoat unbuttoned. His trousers, the colour of treacle, looked like something an outdoor adventurer would wear. His face was weather–beaten but in an attractive, manly sense. Although his skin was pale he had a healthy, outdoors look. The blue of his eyes was as clear as a turquoise sea and emphasised by long dark lashes.

He'd yet to speak, to smile, but the breadth of his chest made me think that his tone would be deep.

He lingered for a moment, looking at me. I felt he'd appraised all five–foot–three of me. Was that a flicker of approval? Did I fit the bill that I was supposed to be?

'I need a cake.' He said it as if it was a burden, an annoyance to him.

I was correct about his tone — deep, polite, Scottish.

I bit back my immediate response that he needed an attitude adjustment when coming into a tearoom or shop. So I said, 'What type of cake? A Victoria sponge? A Battenberg? A birthday cake?'

He wandered over to my window display and eyed the cakes, especially the birthday cake iced with fondant. 'A novelty cake. It's for my business. I'm having a special promotion. I've been advised to have a cake.'

'What's the theme you need for the cake?'

'Bees.'

I pointed to the bees I'd painted into the decor. 'Like those?'

His blue eyes widened and he went over and studied the bees I'd painted on to the tearoom wall along with roses and other flowers.

'There's an old hive in the garden and I painted bees on the walls as part of the decor.'

He spun around and stared at me. 'Where's the hive?'

I went to the patio doors. 'Out the back, opposite the shed. I've only just opened the tearoom. In fact, you're my first official customer. I'm going to sort out the garden once the spring arrives.'

'Can I have a look at the hive?'

'There's nothing in it,' I assured him.

He stood peering out at it so I opened the doors and he went into the garden to study the hive as if it was gold dust.

I waited inside, keeping an eye on the tearoom and at the beehive inquisitor.

'I plan to give the hive a coat of paint in the spring,' I called to him. 'A nice buttery yellow or eggshell blue.'

Satisfied that the hive was long abandoned, he came back over to me. 'I'm interested in the hive. I'd like to buy it. How much do you want for it?'

'I wasn't planning on selling it. I think it adds a nice feature to the garden. And it's authentic.'

'Oh it's authentic all right. It hasn't been occupied for a long time but once a hive has been used, it can be used again.' He glanced back at it. 'I'd really like to buy it, but can I leave it where it is for the moment?'

'I suppose so. You seem very interested in beehives. What is it you do?'

'I'm a beemaster.'

'A beemaster? Is that like a beekeeper extraordinaire?' I asked lightly.

He nodded.

'If the hive is of use you're welcome to have it.'

'Thank–you. How much?'

'No charge, but I'd appreciate it if you'd spread the word about the tearoom and the novelty cake I'll make for you.'

He almost smiled. 'So you're going to make me a beehive cake?'

'Complete with bees flying around it if you want.'

'You can do that?'

'Sort of. I'll stick little fondant bees on thin wires into the cake as if they're flying around the hive.'

I showed him some of the novelty cakes I'd made. I had a portfolio of cake photographs that he could flick through. I'd made cakes shaped like shoes and handbags, a train for a children's party, and lots of other novelty themed cakes.

'I'll have a beehive cake, with bees,' he said and paid for it upfront. 'I need it four days from now.'

'I'll phone when it's ready.'

He noticed the jars of rose petal jam and other conserves on the counter. 'Would you consider selling some jars of my honey?'

'Yes, drop a few in when you collect your cake.'

'Okay. It's been a great yield recently. And very flavoursome. Every year is different depending on where the bees collect from.

11

People have been planting more bee friendly flowers and plants in their gardens within the area of the city and this has helped.'

'The bees are in the city?'

'Yes. The hives are in various locations within the city area.'

'Urban bees?' There was something about the concept, and about the beemaster that felt quite romantic, like someone from a bygone era.

'Yes, I've also got hives in the outskirts.'

'You must be a busy man. A busy bee.'

'Very busy. I'll expect your call.' He handed me a business card. 'This is my mobile number. Phone anytime. I work all sorts of crazy hours.'

'I know how that feels.'

'Are you running this venture on your own?'

'Yes.' I shrugged. 'Circumstances have worked out like that, but I'm going to give it a go. I love baking.'

'I'll spread the word that you're here.'

'I'd appreciate that.'

He picked up one of the little menu cards that I'd printed for customers. 'Hazel...'

The sound of his voice, murmuring my name, resonated through me, through the tearoom, and left me with an impression of the beemaster that was difficult to forget.

For the next hour my thoughts kept drifting back to him, those gorgeous turquoise eyes, fit build and his unusual occupation. A beemaster. Hmmm... What a sweet temptation he was. Not that I was hoping to find romance, not while the bitter aftertaste of Jason still remained. But a woman could dream, couldn't she? Or perhaps that was just asking for trouble.

'Do you make wedding cakes?' a woman said walking up to the counter.

I nodded. 'I do.'

'Our daughter is getting married soon,' the man who was with her explained. 'We had a cake ordered but she's changed her mind. She wants something else. Something more traditional.'

'Shevonne is into vintage,' said the mother. 'She couldn't give a rat's arse about it when we ordered the original cake which was made in the shape of a high–heel shoe. She wanted a fashionista theme to the wedding.'

'Now after nearly two years of planning the wedding reception, she's after a vintage cake.' The father shrugged. 'It's her big day. I want it to be perfect for my wee lassie.'

I flicked through my portfolio of cakes. 'This one is very traditional. Three tiers, white icing, fruit cake, classic piping and fondant tea roses on the top.'

'Oh that's just what we had in mind, isn't it Bert?'

He nodded enthusiastically. 'It is, Bridie. That would be fantastic.' He looked at me. 'Have you got one?'

I wanted to jump up and down. I did. 'I have. It's in the kitchen. I'll bring it through so you can see it.'

I lifted it on to my silver trolley and wheeled it through. I sensed an imaginary fanfare playing when they saw it.

'We'll take it,' said Bridie.

'Yes, definitely.' Bert couldn't wait to get his wallet out to pay for it. Money didn't seem to be an issue, but I charged the usual fair price.

'Cheers for that,' said Bridie. 'What's your name?'

'Hazel.'

'Cheers, Hazel. You've saved us hunting around for a cake.'

Bert hurried out. 'I'll get it in the back of the van.'

A van was parked outside. Some sort of builders van.

I helped them out with the cake. I'd wrapped it in a large white cardboard cake box and tied it with white ribbon.

He opened the rear doors of the van and went to put the cake inside. The van was empty.

'It could get damaged if it falls about in the back,' I said.

'My wife will keep a tight grip on it. Won't you, hen?'

'It won't shoogle while I've got my hands on it,' she said with fierce determination as she climbed into the rear of the van and sat down on the floor.

Fair enough I thought. These people obviously adored their daughter.

'So is this a new tearoom and bakery you've opened up yourself?' said Bert.

'It is. I'm hoping it'll work. When it's warmer I'll have the patio doors open and customers can sit outside in the garden.'

'Yes, I noticed you've got a wee shed out the back,' he said.

'I know the shed's a bit decrepit but I'm thinking of giving it a lick of paint when the weather's better.'

He nodded and smiled. 'Thanks again for the smashing cake. We'll spread the word about your new tearoom.'

I waved them off with their wedding cake.

Two substantial cake sales. Not bad for a frosty morning in late January.

I finished making the beemaster's cake in two days. I'd handcrafted each bee and stuck them on fine wires around the cake. I snapped a photograph of it for my portfolio. The cake was made in three layers of vanilla sponge with buttercream filling and covered with pale yellow icing. I'd added a few flowers around the base and on top. His business card had a logo and I used an edible ink pen in chocolate to draw the bee from the logo on to the cake. Just a little added extra to personalise his cake.

The tearoom had been reasonably busy and I'd made a tiny profit. I was knackered from all the hours I had to work, but now that it was February I hoped that the forecast of an early spring would encourage people to pop in for tea and cakes as the days became brighter.

I found the beemaster's card in the kitchen drawer and while the tearoom was quiet I phoned him.

'Is that August?'

'Yes.'

'This is Hazel. Your cake is ready for collection.'

'That was quick. I'll pick it up later. What time do you close?'

He sounded busy and windblown. I could hear the wind in the background and pictured him outdoors wrestling his bees or whatever it was that he did with them.

'I close at five but I'll be working in the kitchen until about seven. Ring the bell and here's my mobile number in case I'm in the store cupboard and don't hear you.' I reeled off the number.

'Great. I'm extremely busy at the moment so I'll come round this evening.'

August arrived that evening in February.

I'd felt the need to tidy my hair and wear my most attractive apron that gave my slim build a shapely waistline. Some days I forgot to eat properly and running around from early morning until quite late at night every day had taken its toll on my already slender figure.

I'd scrubbed the kitchen, prepared some of the baking for the following morning and planned to put my feet up after giving August the beemaster his cake. I hoped he'd like it.

He rang the doorbell and I went through to let him in.

Oh my goodness he looked handsome standing there, towering above me, wearing his dark greatcoat and weather–beaten boots that added another inch to his height.

He wasn't smiling and I wondered if his serious expression hid a man who had a great sense of humour or whether this was his usual demeanour.

'Can I come in?' he asked.

I blushed, realising I'd been staring at him rather than inviting him inside. 'Yes, sorry...it's been a hectic day. I've got your cake in the kitchen.' I scurried away to get it with the intention of wheeling it through on my silver trolley but he followed me into the kitchen.

'I've got your cake through here.' It was in the storeroom.

I carried it through. The bees wobbled on the wires as I put it down on the kitchen table.

'What do you think? Will it do?'

'This is marvellous.' His stunning blue eyes looked at me sending a tingle through me. 'You've even put my logo on it. How did you do that?'

'I used a chocolate ink pen. It's edible.'

'You've put a lot of work into it. This will impress them at the party.'

'A special promotion is it?'

'Yes, I detest things like that. It's all fuss and falseness. I can't be bothered with that sort of nonsense. I'd rather be working with my bees but business deals rely on PR parties.' He looked at the cake. 'This is brilliant. Thank you, Hazel.'

I smiled at him and put the cake into a box and tied it with gold ribbon.

'Do you bake everything yourself?' he said, looking round at my pristine kitchen which had seemed so much larger until his tall, broad–shouldered stature stood in the midst of it.

'Eh, yes. Cakes, scones, tea bread...everything.'

'You must be busy.'

'Oh yes.'

'Don't you have anyone to help you?'

'Not at the moment. Perhaps once it gets really busy I'll hire someone to help me.'

'Did you just think...I'll have a tearoom and bakery with no thought of how you'd cope running a business like this by yourself?' There was no praise in his voice for my achievement, only a slightly snippy tone insinuating that I hadn't thought things through properly. I was prone to such things, but I felt inclined to explain how I came to be in this position.

'Did your ex–boyfriend really look like a gnome?'

'The resemblance was uncanny. But as I explained to Officer Doyle, my ex was taller. Not as tall as Doyle or you. You're taller than both of them.' And more handsome and sexy, though I supposed Doyle could be a close second and I'd always loved a man in uniform. But the greatcoat August wore gave him a manly, adventurous look.

'So what do you plan to do now?' he said.

'Eh...have a cup of tea after you leave and watch something on the television.'

He almost laughed. 'No, I meant, what's your business plan for the coming months?'

'Oh, well...I plan to make a fair living out of the business and live in the flat upstairs. I'd like to hire a couple of staff by the summer so that I can spend more time creating and decorating the cakes.'

'What about...other things? Do you plan to concentrate on your career or are you hoping to marry and settle down sometime?'

'I've never been lucky when it comes to love.'

He nodded and didn't comment. Then he glanced over at the kettle and teapot.

'Is there any chance of a cup of tea?'

'Yes, I'll put the kettle on. Would you like something with your tea? A slice of cake, a buttered scone with whipped cream and strawberry jam?'

'Thanks, that would be great.'

I got the feeling he hadn't eaten dinner so I cut a generous wedge of Victoria sponge cake, served up a fruit scone, butter, cream and jam, and gave him one of the tomato salad sandwiches I'd made for my dinner.

He took his coat off, put it over the back of his chair and made my heart rate soar when I saw the breadth of his shoulders in his shirt. The shirt had a vintage quality to it, or perhaps it was August who gave the clothes he wore the look of a bygone era. Either way, he looked classy and handsome sitting in my kitchen tucking into his food.

I ate the other sandwich and sipped my tea. He drank his tea and I poured another cup for him.

Then a look of realisation shot across his face. He pointed at the remnants of the sandwich that he was munching. 'This is your dinner, isn't it?'

'Maybe. Luckily, I own a tearoom so there's no shortage of tasty snacks.'

He smiled and held my gaze. 'Thanks for sharing your dinner with me. It's very kind of you.'

'Did you bring any jars of your honey?'

'Damn, I forgot to put them in the car. I meant to bring them. There have been so many things to organise recently.'

'For your promotion?'

'Yes, and after the winter the hives need sorting out. It's going to be an early spring.'

'Yes, so I read. I'm looking forward to it. It's been a long winter, or perhaps it's just me.'

'A difficult winter?' he said gently.

I nodded. 'Harassment, heartache, worry about whether I could make this work on my own. Oh yes. A difficult winter. Roll on springtime.'

'And summer. I love working with the hives in the summer. The bees...the flowers...long summer evenings...it's what I enjoy. It's supposed to be a scorcher this year.'

'I hope so. It would be ideal for the tearoom. I'd like to use the patio and garden for customers to sit outside. And I want to start a vegetable patch growing lettuce and things that I can use for the cooking.'

'I'll come by in the summer and enjoy a relaxing tea in the garden.' He said this as if he wouldn't see me again for months. I pushed all wild notions of seeing August on a regular basis from my mind.

'Tell me about your bees. What do you do?'

He finished eating a mouthful of sponge cake and began spreading jam on his scone. 'I tend to the hives, making sure they're looked after properly. Sometimes the hives become damaged either by the weather or people interfere with them. I basically keep them ticking over while the bees produce their harvest of honey. Then I collect the honey and market it. I also give talks on beekeeping and other stuff related to that. The hives are situated in various locations so it's rather like keeping a lot of plates spinning at the one time without letting any of them fall.'

'How did you become a beemaster?'

'My grandfather was a beemaster and when I was a boy I used to spend the summer at my grandparents house and learned everything I needed to know from the master himself. I've travelled the world since then and learned from other beemasters.'

'Do you ever get stung?'

'Yes, but not too often and I'm used to it. Working with bees, I wear the right clothing and use the right equipment. I'm very careful when I handle the hives and I'm gentle with my bees.'

'You obviously love what you do.'

He nodded. 'Unfortunately it leaves very little time for anything else. I suppose I'm like you. Unlucky in love, especially when I'm too busy for a proper relationship. Women have no time for a busy man.'

August's phone rang. He glanced at the caller's name and frowned. 'I have to go. What do I owe you for dinner?' He got up, shrugged his coat on and picked up the cake box.

'Nothing for dinner.'

'Are you sure?' he said.

'You've already paid for the cake.'

He nodded, smiled and hurried out of the kitchen.

I unlocked the front door and he stepped outside.

'I'll have someone drop the honey off to you tomorrow,' he called to me and got into his car. 'Thanks again, Hazel.'

I watched him drive off wondering if I'd ever see him again. I went through to the kitchen, cleaned up the tea dishes and then went upstairs.

18

I kept thinking about August and those gorgeous turquoise eyes of his, so to take my mind off the effect he had on me, I added up my sales. The plain and fruit scones had both sold well but the surprise success was my treacle scones. The traditional Victoria sponges had gone down a treat and a few customers commented that they loved the generous amount of jam and cream filling. I'd sold a silver wedding anniversary cake to a couple who'd only come in to buy soda scones. And I'd had an order for a vintage novelty cake with pink and white iced bunting so I planned to work on that in the morning.

All in all a productive day — and night. I closed my accounts file and flopped back on the sofa. That's when I heard the doorbell ringing downstairs.

I jumped up and peered out the living room window that had a view of the street.

What was he doing here at this time of night?

CHAPTER THREE

Battenberg and Hazelnut Cake

Officer Doyle stood outside the tearoom — and he wasn't alone.

Through the glass front door I saw the figure standing beside him, and my heart sank. The gnome was back.

I opened the door and waited for an explanation.

'I was doing my usual drive through the area at night,' said Doyle, 'and I saw that your friend was back. Someone's stuck a note to his hat. I saw your lights were on upstairs, so I thought I'd chap your door and let you know.'

I glared down at the gnome.

'It's definitely him,' said Doyle. 'I checked the dent in his arse. Someone must've wanted rid of him before you inherited him.'

I confessed that I'd inflicted the dent the night Jason told me he was leaving me and was involved with someone else. I'd taken my anger out on his plastic lookalike and booted it halfway across the garden at the back of the tearoom. If Jason hadn't done a runner that night so fast it could've been his arse that got the toe of my boot up it.

'I think you should read the note,' said Doyle. 'It's addressed to the woman who owns the tearoom. I can't legally open it and I'm desperate to know what it says.'

'Me too.' I tore the note from his hat, opened it and read the message. 'I saw your gnome when I was out shopping near the markets. I assume someone stole him from your tearoom garden. Nothing is safe these days. I'm pretty sure he belongs to you. He looks the same as the one you had. I used to see that man of yours on his mobile late at night in the garden making furtive phone calls. He always adjusted the gnome before he went back inside. I'm a neighbour. I've not been spying on you. I just happened to notice. I think he really liked the gnome. It had the same hair as him — like corrugated iron. I presume you've been looking for him. The gnome not the man. Anyway, I thought I'd put him on your doorstep. All the luck with your tearoom. Elspeth (two doors down and round the corner).'

'That was very neighbourly of her,' said Doyle.

I sighed. 'It was, wasn't it?'

'Will I take him and fling him at the recycling unit again?'

'Would you mind?'

'Not at all. I'm driving back that way to the station. I'm due my coffee break. I'll drop him off as I go by.'

'Thanks. Would you like a cake to go with your coffee?'

He hesitated, but his expression perked up at my offer.

I went inside and flicked the lamp on above the counter displaying the selection of cakes. That's when I noticed someone had accidentally left a set of house keys on the counter. Obviously they'd left them when paying for their purchases. The key ring was very sparkly and I tried to think of any women who would've left them lying there. I told Doyle who'd stepped inside to choose his cake.

'I'll take the keys with me to the lost property at the station. If anyone comes in to ask about them, tell them you handed them into the police. They can come and collect them at the station.'

He put the set of keys in his pocket.

'Thanks, it's handy that you were here. So...what type of cake would you like? I've got hazelnut cake, chocolate roll, walnut cake, pear and plum sponge, cherry Madeira, Battenberg —'

'Battenberg? That's one of my favourites. I haven't had that in ages.'

I was pleased that I could give him something he liked in thanks for helping me with the gnome and the keys. I lifted up one of the cakes and went to slice into it.

'No, don't waste your lovely cake, Hazel. Give me a slice of anything you've already cut into.'

I didn't listen to him. I was quite happy to give him the Battenberg. I cut two thick slices and wrapped the rest of the cake up for him as well. 'Here are a couple of slices for your break. And take the other half for later.'

His eyes sparkled in the lamp light. 'That's very kind of you.'

'It's the least I can do.'

Doyle's police car was parked outside. He put the gnome in the front passenger seat and strapped him in with the seat belt. 'It'll save him rattling around in the boot. He's got enough dents in him. No one will want to steal him...I mean...take him home, if he's damaged

21

further. He'll get melted down for sure.' He tightened the strap across the gnome's chest and put the Battenberg cake on the seat beside him. 'Cheers again for the cake.'

'You're welcome, Doyle.'

As he started up the car a message came through on his radio. He had the window rolled down and I overheard them saying, 'There's a break–in reported by neighbours at one of the large mansions up at the crescent. The burglar is still inside the premises. Would all officers within the vicinity make their way there immediately.'

He clicked the reply button. 'Officer Doyle here. I'm only five minutes from there. I'm on my way.'

He waved at me and drove off at speed to the scene of the crime.

I know it was silly of me, but I'd always wanted to be in a high–speed police car in pursuit of...well, anything really. Just for the thrill of the chase. So I resented that of all the ones that was whizzing off in the car it was that ruddy gnome. Typical.

But at least I was rid of him. Again.

I cut a slice of chocolate roll and took it upstairs to have with a late night cup of tea.

The next morning I was up early working in the kitchen baking cakes. A small television sat on a shelf and I'd turned it on feeling it was the nearest thing to company.

The voices droned on in the background and I changed the channels and caught the end of the early morning local news. The newsreader concluded, 'We finish this morning's news with a light–hearted story. Last night police in Glasgow were called to a break–in at a house in the city centre. The first to arrive was a police officer, identified as Officer Doyle, who had a garden gnome strapped into the passenger seat of his police car. Neighbours had alerted the police about a man wearing a long dark coat attempting to shimmy along window ledges and jemmy a bedroom window open on an upstairs property.'

I blinked when I saw footage of the scene. Someone had probably captured it with their phone because it was juddery. But I could see Doyle and lots of people pointing at the car and making jokes and laughing about the gnome.

The newsreader continued, 'Our reporter at the scene overheard Officer Doyle tell a colleague that the gnome belonged to a woman called Hazel who'd opened a tearoom recently in Glasgow and that he recommended her baking.' The newsreader added with a smile, 'Which could account for the gnome having Battenberg cake beside him in the police car.'

They finished with a close–up of the gnome.

I flicked the television off and sat down in the kitchen. I'd been mentioned on the news because of that bloody gnome. Was there no getting rid of him?

The timer pinged on my tin loaves and I took them out of the oven. The crusts had browned nicely.

As the morning wore on a few more customers than usual arrived having heard about me on the news. I kept hoping that Doyle hadn't taken too much of a ribbing about having a gnome with him. Then a police car pulled up outside and two officers got out. My stomach knotted in dread as they walked into the tearoom and stared straight at me.

They didn't look as friendly as Doyle.

One of them headed to the back of the tearoom sussing the place out while the other approached the counter. I almost squished the fairy cake I had in my hand that was ready for its silvery sprinkles.

'Is your name Hazel?' the officer said.

My heart was thundering in my chest. Hell's bells — what had I done?

I nodded.

His cold blue eyes scanned the cakes in the display counter and then travelled back up to me.

'Can we have two Battenbergs, four cream cakes, whatever you recommend, and two dozen mixed scones? Plenty of treacle ones.'

At first I didn't register his order, then a sense of relief washed over me and I smiled. 'Would you like a couple of big soda scones with that? They're fresh baked this morning.'

'Aye. Sling them in the bag as well.'

The other officer came and joined us. 'I see you've got the coal fire on.'

My smile froze. Had I broken some fire law I didn't know about?

'Any chance of a cuppa and a cake over there before we head back to the station?' he said.

'Take a seat and make yourselves comfy officers. I'll bring a pot of tea for two over in a minute.'

23

They went over and sat down, heating their hands at the fire. It was a blistering cold day. I guessed that despite the fiasco with Doyle and the gnome, the cake had gone down well at the police station.

I served up their tea and two iced buns filled with cream.

'Doyle recommended your tearoom,' said the first officer. 'It's handy to have somewhere like this on our route.'

The other nodded as he bit into an iced bun.

'You're always welcome, and you can phone in orders ahead and I'll have them ready for you to pick up if you're in a hurry.'

'Perfect,' said the second officer. He held up the remainder of his bun. 'This is like old–fashioned home baking. Stuff you can really get your teeth into.'

I smiled and left them to finish their tea while I served other customers.

About fifteen minutes later, the police paid for their order and went to leave. I ran after them with their change.

They brushed it aside. 'Ach, you're fine, Hazel,' one of them said. 'And thanks for the tea.'

And off they went, leaving me with a generous tip.

For the first time ever, the four sewing machines at the back of the tearoom were occupied and being used by customers who'd popped in for tea. I noticed that they'd all come equipped with their sewing bags. Spools of thread were being wound, pinking shears clipping away. They appeared to know each other and were working diligently on a quilt, a tea cup holder and judging from the pattern beside one of the tables a blanket for a cat's basket. They'd moved their tea and fairy cakes over to the sewing area. One woman, similar in age and build to me, with shiny brown hair and a lovely fresh complexion, was sewing an apron. A vintage style apron. I craned to see the pattern. I really liked the look of it.

She caught me staring and waved, then she came over to the counter, bringing the apron with her. She seemed quite an unassuming person but she had a pretty smile and appeared genuinely happy to approach me.

'I hope it's okay to use the sewing machines. We heard that you'd made them available for customers. We've bought tea and cakes.' She explained that she was with her Aunt Janetta and two other ladies who liked to sew.

'Yes, that's what they're for.' I glanced at the apron she was twisting nervously in her hands. 'I love your apron. I was trying to see what pattern you were using.'

She ran away and came back with it in seconds. She was certainly skeich.

'It's an old pattern from the 1940s. It belonged to my mum. She used to sew all her own clothes.' She showed me the fabric she'd used for the apron. It was a ditsy floral print.

'It's very nice,' I said. 'I bought remnants of floral fabric to make aprons that I can wear in the tearoom. I enjoy sewing myself, but I haven't had time to work on them yet.'

'Oh well...would you like me and the ladies to run you up two or three aprons?' she offered.

'I eh...'

'I've nothing else to sew at the moment. This apron is for my job. I work four nights a week in a restaurant kitchen but I prefer to use my own aprons. If you've got the fabric give it to us and we'll get started.'

'The fabric is upstairs in my flat.'

'I'll hold the fort while you go and get it. I've always worked in restaurants and cafes. You'll only be a minute anyway.'

I ran upstairs, grabbed the bag filled with fabric remnants and matching thread, and gave it to...I didn't even know her name.

'I'm Elspeth,' she said, taking me by surprise.

Elspeth the gnome rescuer?

'I brought your gnome back.' She looked around. 'Where is he? Someone said he'd been featured on this morning's news but I think they were kidding me on.'

'No, he was on the news and is now...in police custody. The officer involved is handling the gnome situation.'

Her light brown eyes were wide with curiosity. 'It just shows you what gnomes can get up to, doesn't it?'

'Oh definitely,' I said.

Her attention swung towards the fabrics. 'Is that the material?'

I showed her the various pieces of linen and cotton. Roses, lavender and mixed floral designs on cream backgrounds were the main colours. 'I bought several remnants that looked like they had a vintage floral pattern. I thought they'd be ideal for aprons. As I say, I haven't had time to sew them.'

She clasped the bag and smiled like someone who'd been given a worthwhile mission. 'Leave them with us. We'll sort out your apron shortage.' She glanced at me. 'You're about the same size as me. We're a bit on the slim side,' she said, and then her face broke into a smile. 'All the more room for cream cakes.'

While Elspeth and the ladies began their mission with gusto, I refilled their teapots and put down another round of scones with cream and raspberry jam. Their faces lit up. I wasn't sure how much they'd charge for sewing the aprons, but I wondered if they'd be willing to do an exchange today. Free tea and scones in exchange for their sewing skills.

During the next hour the number of customers practically doubled and I was run off my feet trying to serve at the counter and attend to the tables. I was coping — just. But that's when an attractive and well–dressed young woman in her late twenties came sauntering in carrying a cardboard box. She put the box down on the counter. Perfectly made up eyes outlined with liner evaluated me coldly.

'August asked me to drop off his honey. There are twenty–four jars, three flavours, and a price list in the box. He'll go fifty–fifty with you on all sales.' Without giving me a chance to comment, she added, 'August also wants to know if he left his keys lying on the counter. They were on a sparkly key ring.'

'Those were August's keys?'

'Yes, they're his house keys. He's always dropping them in the grass when working with the bees so he uses a sparkly key ring as it's easier to see them.'

'I didn't know who the keys belonged to. I handed them to the police. He can collect them from lost property. Ask for Officer Doyle. He's knows about them.'

'It would've been handier if you'd held on to them, but I suppose I can collect them at the police station.' She sounded as if this was such an annoyance and glared at me to hammer home the point.

'At least his keys are safe,' I said.

She pushed her silky blond hair back from her face. 'He'll be pleased that he doesn't have to climb up and break into his own house again tonight.'

'He broke into his house?'

'Yes, and neighbours reported him to the police thinking he was a burglar. It was on the news. But I suppose you were too busy baking whatever it is you make to notice. Anyway, there's the honey. I'm off to get August's keys.'

'Who are you by the way?' I called to her as she strutted out in a pair of tight jeans that made me wince uncomfortably.

She heard me but chose to ignore my question. If this was August's girlfriend he needed someone else to do his PR for him.

'It looked like her arse was chewing those jeans of hers,' Elspeth's Aunt Janetta remarked. She had a loosely tacked apron in her hands. 'I wanted to see if this would sit comfortably around your waist and to find the best position for the pockets.'

Janetta wrapped the apron around me, judged that it fitted well and put pins where she thought the pockets should be. A few customers looked on in amusement, mildly entertained by the sewing. 'Ideal. I'll run it up in the machine. I do love sewing items like these.'

Another rush of customers invaded the tearoom. I tried to keep on top of things but even I had to admit that I could do with a helping hand. I wondered if I should pin up a notice in the window. *Part–time tearoom assistant wanted. Flexible hours*. Or something like that.

I'd barely thought this through when a young man, tall and slim, walked into the tearoom. He had a scrubbed appearance, very clean, slightly old–fashioned, tidy brown hair, twinkly blue eyes and an open smile that made me want to like him.

'Hello,' he said to me, extending his hand. 'I'm Kevin. I can bake anything.'

CHAPTER FOUR

The Old Beehive

'I noticed how busy you are,' said Kevin, 'and I wondered if you were looking for someone to help you.' His face was bright with enthusiasm.

I continued to serve customers while talking to Kevin. 'I haven't been open long and I'm not really in a financial position to employ anyone but I suppose...'

He cut–in and smiled at me. 'You wouldn't need to employ me, Hazel. I'm self–employed. I'm twenty–nine and have been working for myself since last year. I've worked in lots of cafes and restaurants but I want to hire myself out as a baking expert. I work part–time in a bar. I'm a whiz at making cocktails, but baking is where my heart lies. But it's not easy finding a job where I can experiment with my cake recipes. I like all the old–fashioned stuff that my granny used to make, but most places I've worked only want modern fancy cakes — and that's just not my style. One day, I'd like to own my own cake business, but I've things that I want to learn before I do that. And make enough money to do it which I don't have at the moment.'

I nodded, taking in everything he was telling me.

'You could start by hiring me for an hour or two a day a few days a week. I don't charge a lot and I'd be happy to come to some arrangement with you. My hours are flexible but I work at nights at the bar. I live just down the road.' He pointed out the window. 'I live with my parents. I saw you taking your gnome for a walk late at night recently. You went past my window.'

'I wasn't taking the gnome for a walk. I was...never mind.' I thought about Kevin's offer. It seemed reasonable. But could he really bake?

That question was swiftly answered when a customer came in and asked for a dozen plain scones.

'I'm sorry,' I said, 'but I've no plain scones left. They're sold out.'

Kevin dived into the conversation, giving me a glazed look as if to say, please don't contradict me. 'There's a batch of plain scones due to be put into the oven, Hazel. They'll be ready in less than half an hour.' He smiled at the customer. 'If you've any shopping to do, you could pick them up on your way back. Or come in and have a cuppa and a chocolate cream slice while they're baking.'

The customer looked longingly at the chocolate cream slice that Kevin pointed to.

'There's a seat by the fire,' said Kevin. 'Give yourself a wee treat.'

The customer was already nodding and let herself be escorted over to the table.

I sorted a pot of tea for her and put a chocolate cream slice on a plate. 'I don't have any scones ready,' I whispered to Kevin.

'I'm on it,' he said.

'But...'

'Trust me, Hazel. I know my way around *any* kitchen.'

'The flour for the scones is in the cupboard beside the pantry. Use the big mixer. It's set up with the mixing bowl. Clean trays are in the first oven.' I reeled off the instructions at speed.

I was still giving Kevin instructions as he hurried away, disappearing into the kitchen. I served up the tea and chocolate cream slice and peeked in at him washing his hands before he started to work like blazes making the scones.

Ten minutes later Kevin emerged from the kitchen wearing one of my white aprons that was hanging on the pantry door. 'The scones will be ready soon.'

'That was fast,' I said.

'I'm fast at everything I do. Even as a wee boy I was hyper. It used to annoy the teachers at school but it comes in handy as an adult when I need to get a lot of work done.'

He went over to chat to the customer about their scones. I overheard them chatting about baking. 'Yes,' said Kevin, '

Hazel's brilliant. I love the look of the tearoom. You'll have to try one of her Victoria sponge cakes.' The timer pinged on the oven. 'That'll be your scones ready. I'll let them cool a bit and then you can have them fresh baked from the oven.'

The woman looked delighted and sat by the fire drinking her tea as Kevin disappeared again into the kitchen.

29

Elspeth came over and said to me, 'Was that Kevin? Is he working here now?'

'It is, and he seems to be.'

'Kevin lives just down the road. He can bake anything,' she confided.

'Is he okay?' I said.

'Yes, there's nothing furtive about Kevin. What you see is what you get. He's a nice fella.'

The customer left with their scones and also purchased a Victoria sponge.

Yes, I was keeping Kevin.

The tearoom was busy during the afternoon and I was glad I had Kevin to help me — and Elspeth. Having started the day working on my own, I had acquired two part–time, freelance staff. Elspeth had finished sewing my apron and when I got busy at the counter serving customers, Elspeth came over to help. She wasn't an expert baker like Kevin but having someone to tend the shop counter was so handy.

Elspeth's aunt and the sewing ladies had finished the aprons. Now that there were three of us working in the tearoom the extra aprons were useful.

The ladies started to sew a jelly roll quilt while the world of the tearoom swirled happily around them.

'I can sew,' Kevin commented as he arranged August's jars of honey in the display counter.

'Really?' I said.

He mumbled and fussed with the honey. 'Well...I can sometimes sew a button on my shirt.' He lifted up his tie to reveal that he had a button missing on his shirt. 'I'll get a needle and thread and sew it back on later.' He had the button tucked into his shirt pocket. 'It pinged off last night.'

Elspeth gave me a wink. 'Lost a button last night, eh, Kevin? What were you up to?'

We laughed.

'I wasn't up to what you two are insinuating,' he said. 'Though that would be worth losing a button for.'

My ex would beg to differ.

'We'll sew that back on for you,' Elspeth told him. She led him by the arm over to her Aunt Janetta and friends.

'Kevin needs a button sewn on his shirt,' she announced.

The quilting was put aside and Kevin was smothered by the women who had the shirt off his back in seconds.

Kevin stood there in his thermal vest and the white apron.

There was a lot of teasing and giggling going on from the women and customers who were up for some light–hearted banter.

'You've got more muscle on you than I thought you'd have,' Elspeth remarked and gave his wiry bicep a squeeze.

'It's all the baking and working at the bar — and the cleaning up. I know I look like a long drink of water with my clothes on, but I'm lean and fit as a whippet.'

We were laughing at Kevin when Doyle walked into the tearoom.

'Diversifying?' he said to me, eyeing Kevin in his vest.

'He lost a button off his shirt,' I explained. 'The ladies are sewing it on for him.'

Amid all the explanations, I noticed Elspeth gazing at Doyle. He looked particularly handsome in his uniform under the tearoom lights. She looked interested in him so I introduced them.

'This is Officer Doyle.'

'Pleased to meet you,' she said smiling at him.

'And this is...*Elspeth.*'

He recognised the name immediately. He smiled and nodded at her.

Was that a spark of attraction I saw between them?

'I'm always losing a button off my uniform shirts.' He pulled his jacket open to show that he had one missing. 'I lost that one this morning.'

'Were you wrestling a dangerous criminal?' said Elspeth.

'No, I was typing up a report and it pinged off and hit the computer screen. I managed to find it. I'll stitch it on tonight. You've got to keep your uniform tidy.'

'I could sew it on for you, Officer Doyle,' Elspeth offered.

'Thanks for the offer, Elspeth.' He glanced at Kevin and spoke up so that he could hear. 'But I won't stand with my shirt off in the tearoom while all the women gawp at me.'

31

Kevin hurried up and put his shirt back on. Janetta had sewn the button on for him.

Elspeth stepped closer to Doyle. 'I could sew your button on for you, officer. You wouldn't have to take your shirt off if you didn't mind me handling your shirt while you're wearing it.'

She waited on his response. And so did I. Elspeth was blushing and flirting with Doyle.

He hesitated but I saw a flicker of interest in his eyes. Yes, there was a spark between them.

'I can sew a button on in less than fifty seconds,' Elspeth said to him.

'In that case...' He let her sew the button on his shirt.

I think everyone in the tearoom was fascinated by the innocent yet seductive way she slid her hand inside his shirt to prevent sticking the needle in him while she sewed the button on.

'There,' she said, smoothing her hand down his shirt after buttoning it up. 'That didn't even take a minute.'

I left them to flirt with each other while I dealt with the customers. I didn't even notice Doyle leave. Elspeth came over to me. 'That policeman was lovely.'

'Did he ask you out?' I said.

'No.' Her voice was high-pitched. 'I'm just saying he was lovely.'

Kevin nudged her. 'You were flirting with him.'

'I was not.'

'You definitely were,' I told her.

'He seemed interested,' said Kevin.

Elspeth looked flattered. 'Really? Was he? I love a man in uniform.'

'At least if he loses a button while he's with you,' I said, 'you'll be able to sew it back on again.'

Bert came in looking for more silver favours for his daughter's wedding cake.

'It's pandemonium at the house. Bridie's sorting things out but Shevonne's excited about her big day tomorrow and fretting about everything including the cake favours, so I thought I'd drive over and buy a few extra to keep her happy.'

I handed him a small box of assorted favours. 'There are plenty in the box for her to choose from.'

He paid for them and smiled at me. 'Cheers, Hazel.'

I waved him off. 'Good luck with the wedding tomorrow.'

He waved back and drove off in his builders van.

After closing Kevin helped me clean up the kitchen.

'Thanks for taking a chance on me,' he said. 'I appreciate the work.'

'I'm glad of the help,' I said, preparing a plate of sandwiches for my dinner.

Kevin frowned at them. 'Is that your dinner?'

'Yes, just for easiness tonight.'

He shook his head. 'You have to eat right, Hazel. You can't live on sandwiches.'

'I plan to eat right once I've settled in with the business. Tonight I just want to go upstairs and relax with a cuppa.'

He took his apron off and put his jacket on to leave. 'I have to get going. The bar is always jumping on a Friday night. I'll drop by tomorrow and give you a hand with the cake baking.'

I smiled. 'See you tomorrow.'

Before he left he said, 'I don't want to rake over the old coals, but I heard about your ex–boyfriend dumping you and leaving you to get on with this business alone. But you're better off without him, Hazel.'

And then he left.

I locked the door behind him and gazed out at the early evening sky. It wasn't as dark as it had been. The nights were becoming lighter. I was looking forward to the spring, the milder evenings and crisp fresh mornings.

I glanced at the jars of honey on the counter before switching off the lamp. I'd asked Doyle if the woman August sent with the honey had collected his house keys. Doyle confirmed that she had and that her name was Charliss. She was August's assistant. And perhaps a lot more than that?

The little solar lights flickered in the garden. I went over to the patio doors and peered out at the ramshackle shed. I reckoned it would take more than a coat of pastel paint to make it look attractive. If the weather was mild on Sunday I planned to tackle the garden, pulling out the weeds and spindly bushes that looked like they hadn't bloomed in years. I quite enjoyed gardening and the high wall around the edges gave a hidden quality to it, like a haven within the heart of the city, a niche that could be made into a lovely cottage–style garden and an extension of the tearoom. There was a pear tree tucked into the far corner and if nurtured properly it might yield some fruit in the summer.

And there was the old beehive waiting to be collected by August.

I took my sandwiches and one of the plain scones Kevin had made that was left over and went upstairs. I was so exhausted I didn't finish all the sandwiches but I ate Kevin's scone which was light and delicious and drank a whole pot of tea. Tomorrow was Saturday and there was every chance that the tearoom would be busy, especially if the weather was fine and brought people into the city to do their shopping.

Gazing out at the night sky it looked like a mild day was due. There were no clouds in the sky and the lights from the city sparkled in the clear evening air. Bert and Bridie's daughter was getting married in the morning and her wedding reception was being held in one of the hotels in the city centre. I hoped the extra favours would make the cake everything they wanted it to be for their daughter's special day.

CHAPTER FIVE

Wedding Cake Chaos

It was a bright sunny morning and I was assembling my double layer Victoria sponge cakes when Kevin arrived.

'Is that plum jam you're spreading on the Victoria sponges?'

I held up the jar. 'Yes, plum jam but only on the top layer. I put raspberry jam on the bottom and cream on both. When I make the double sponges I use two types of jam. The plum jam has a mild taste but it really makes the flavour of the raspberry jam pop.'

'I must try that,' said Kevin, putting on one of the flowery aprons Elspeth and the sewing ladies had made.

He looked at the ovens full of baking. 'What would you like me to give you a hand with?'

'The treacle scones are due out any minute. You could put them out to cool and then make a start on the next batch. And are you okay about making mocha cake? Or would you prefer to tackle the walnut cake?'

'I'll tackle both and let you get on with something else.'

'Great. I thought with it being Saturday I'd make chocolate fudge cakes and cut them up into large wedges.'

We worked well together and chatted about Kevin's ex-girlfriends, that none of them could bake, and how he loved to search the market stalls for unusual cake tins and vintage bakeware.

Soon it was time to open the tearoom.

I'd just unlocked the front door and was wheeling the pink bicycle out to put it on display to attract customers when Elspeth arrived. Her coat was unbuttoned and her scarf blew around her shoulders as she hurried towards me.

'Sorry I'm a wee bit late but I met Doyle in the street and we got chatting.'

I put the bicycle in front of the window and secured it with a bike lock.

'Chatting to Doyle?' I smiled at her. 'Has he asked you out yet?'

She flapped the ends of her scarf and pretended that there was no reason for him to be asking her out. 'We were just talking. Nothing more.'

We went inside and Kevin started to wind her up. 'You're blushing, Elspeth. I think you fancy Officer Doyle.'

'I'm not blushing. My face is flushed from running down the road.'

I exchanged a smile with Kevin.

The tearoom started to get busy. I put more coal on the fire and kept pace with the baking, as did Kevin, while Elspeth manned the counter.

I made pots of tea while she watched how much tea I added to each pot and the blends I used.

'The tea you made me and the ladies yesterday was very refreshing,' said Elspeth. 'What type was it?'

'That was what I call the house tea,' I explained. 'Heat the teapot, then add three parts of the loose leaf regular tea. It's a popular brand. Then add one part Earl Grey. It makes a really refreshing tea. But some customers will want a particular brand.' I pointed to the shelf where numerous types of tea were kept.

Although coffee was available, tea and hot chocolate were the most popular. People seemed to like the old–fashioned cake recipes and the vintage atmosphere of the tearoom and bakery.

At mid–day a phone call came through for me. It was Bert — and he sounded distressed.

'Hazel, it's Bert. I'm phoning from the wedding reception.'

'How did the wedding go?' I said.

'Fine, great, brilliant. But there's been a catastrophe with the cake and I need your help.'

'What happened to the cake?'

'We arrived at the hotel for the reception and the photographer suggested we put the cake out on the balcony so he could get pictures of the happy couple against the blue sky. It's such a nice day. Anyway, Bridie and the bridesmaids were scattering rose petals on Shevonne's dress and arranging her train so that it would look lovely in the photos. But then a dirty big seagull flew over and did a shite right on top of the cake.'

I gasped.

'It's ruined the top layer. A clean hit. The other two layers didn't get shite on them. It wasn't a splatter or anything like that, but Bridie's trying to placate Shevonne and the meal's being held up until we can cut the cake. I didn't know what else to do but phone you and ask — is there anything you can do to replace the top of the cake? It's an emergency situation, Hazel.'

'I'm thinking, I'm thinking,' I muttered, looking at the cakes in the display cabinet. I quickly whispered what had happened to Kevin who relayed it to Elspeth.

'A seagull's done a shite on the wedding cake,' he summarised.

I spoke to Bert. 'I've got a birthday cake that's got traditional white icing and fondant roses and other flowers on the top. It's similar to the wedding cake.'

'That'll do. Can you get it over here pronto?' said Bert. 'I'll pay anything you ask.'

He gave me details of the hotel. It was four blocks away in the city centre and the wedding reception was being held in the main function room.

'I'm on my way,' I said. 'Tell Shevonne I'll sort it. Top her up with champagne or something until I get there.'

'Cheers, Hazel,' said Bert.

I panicked hearing the relief in his voice. They were relying on me. I scrambled around for pillars and favours to help assemble the makeshift cake top.

'Will I phone a taxi?' said Elspeth.

I looked outside. The Saturday lunchtime traffic was gridlocked. I ran outside to see if there was any way I could run with the cake but it was too far. Then I saw the pink bike. Without hesitation I unlocked it and shouted to Kevin. 'Bring the cake out.'

Kevin and Elspeth came rushing out with it. Elspeth had put it in a cake box and then in a carrier bag.

I secured it in the front basket and got on the bike.

'I've put two nozzles, a piping bag and a packet of ready mixed icing in the bag in case you need to tart the cake up,' said Kevin.

'Great,' I said, hoping I could remember how to ride a bike. I hadn't been on a bicycle in years, but it was one of those things you never forget, or so they say.

Elspeth ran in and came back out with my jacket. I threw it on and then sped off.

'Good luck, Hazel,' shouted Kevin.

I peddled like blazes, taking the racing line through gaps in the traffic where a bike could go but cars couldn't. I cut up side streets, through the main city area, down a cobbled lane that made my insides wobble, then powered on towards the hotel. I cast the bike aside and ran with the cake into the reception. Bert was waiting for me at the door waving me on.

Then we both ran to where the cake was sitting in the corner on a buffet table. Catering staff were standing by to help.

I lifted the birthday cake out the bag and Bert actually cheered when it saw it. The size and style was an ideal fit for the top layer. I didn't need the extra pillars. All I had to do was sit it on top. I used one of the nozzles to pipe a few fancy embellishments around the flowers and stuck on four silver favours to make it a better match for the bottom layers. Voila! Sorted.

I was totally exhausted but happily so. Bert almost squeezed the breath out of me, as did his wife when they saw that the wedding cake was ready to be cut and photographed.

They insisted I be included in two of the photographs, and I somehow downed two glasses of pink champagne in the process. A toast to the bride and groom. Phew!

Then I was off on my bike again back to the tearoom.

I parked the bike outside the front window and went inside. The tearoom was busy and Elspeth had asked Janetta to help serve up the teas.

Kevin's face was filled with concern as he approached me. He was carrying a cake stand full of cream scones and lemon drizzle cake to put out on one of the tables.

Kevin whispered anxiously to me, 'There's a man in your garden. He's trying to lift up your beehive.'

'Is it August?'

'No, Hazel, it's February.'

I left Kevin to serve the cakes up and went over and looked out the patio doors. 'August was trying to get his arms round the hive to pull it free from the weeds that had grown around it.'

I went out into the garden. 'Do you want a hand with that?'

August looked round at me. 'Where were you? Your staff didn't believe me when I said that the beehive was mine, that you'd given it to me. They said you'd sped off on your bicycle to fend off a seagull from a wedding reception. What the hell were you doing? Does trouble and chaos always follow you around?'

'No, of course not.' Just sometimes. Unfortunately a lot recently. I didn't dare bring up the subject of his house keys.

But he did. 'I had to break into my own house because I'd left my keys on your shop counter.'

'That wasn't my fault.'

'You should've phoned me instead of calling the police.'

'I didn't call the police. Officer Doyle arrived because he saw the garden gnome outside the tearoom.'

'Oh yes, the gnome. The gnome that looks like your ex–boyfriend. The mind boggles!'

'At least the gnome has slightly more personality than your girlfriend. And why are you picking on me, especially when you're helping yourself to my beehive?'

'What girlfriend? I don't have a girlfriend.'

'She delivered the honey. She fetched your keys from the police station. Doyle said her name was Charliss.'

'She assists with my admin and things like that when I'm busy.'

'I'll just bet she does.'

He stopped wrestling with the hive. 'You sound jealous.'

'I'm not jealous. Why would I be jealous?'

'I don't know. I've heard women's voices with that tone before and it's usually because they're jealous.' He stared at the beehive. 'I'll leave it and come back tomorrow with a shovel to loosen the weeds.'

'Oh for goodness sake,' I said and stomped past him. 'It's only a few weeds.' I ripped them out with my bare hands and then wrapped my arms around the hive to tug it free.

'No, Hazel, don't.'

I put all my strength into it. 'I can feel it start to move. Yes, one more pull and it'll be...'

It was August's own fault that he got winded in the gut. He shouldn't have stood right behind me when I pulled the hive free. It wasn't that heavy, just awkward, though less awkward than August and his hoity–toity attitude.

'Here,' I said, thrusting the hive at him.

His gorgeous eyes looked at me and I sensed that his ego had taken a beating. He'd let a girl lift the hive. That's what the expression on his handsome face told me.

'Thank you,' he said, and then went to carry it into the tearoom.

'No, don't carry it through the tearoom. It's covered in dirt and weeds. I'll open the side gates and you can carry it out to your car.

I had the keys on my key ring. I unlocked the metal gate. August stepped into the path that ran along the side of the premises. I secured the gate again in case any customers wandered out on to the patio and ventured up there.

'I'll open the front gate,' I said to August. 'Hold on a minute.' I went through the tearoom, out the front door and put the key in the metal gate at the front. The lock wouldn't open. It was jammed.

August was holding the hive and glaring through the gate at me. 'Can't you open it?'

I tried to wiggle the key in the lock. 'It's stuck.' And so was the key. The key opened both gates so now August was locked between the two, with the tearoom on one side and a really high wall on the other.

'Oh brilliant,' he said, his tone edged with sarcasm. 'Now I'm stuck here while you go and fetch a jemmy or a ruddy large hammer.'

'I'm not breaking the lock. I need the premises secure at night. I'll phone a locksmith. They come out for emergencies.'

'You sound as if you have prior experience of this sort of thing, though that doesn't surprise me.'

I peered through the bars of the gate at him. 'Is there something up your nose, because you've been nothing but snippy to me since I came out to help you with the beehive?'

I thought he was going to answer, then his sensual mouth tightened into a firm line. Whatever he'd wanted to say he was keeping to himself.

I went inside and told Kevin and Elspeth what had happened. Then I looked up emergency locksmiths in the area. One of them said he'd be there within an hour. I made a cup of tea for August and took it out to him. I balanced a pink macaron on the edge of the saucer.

'The locksmith will be here within the hour. Have a tea to sweeten you up.'

He reluctantly took the tea and then sat down on the hive, cupping the tea and glaring at me as if everything was my fault. Okay, so some of it was my fault but he should've known that a Saturday wasn't the ideal time to collect his hive. The tearoom would obviously be busy with customers. I couldn't let him traipse through carrying a beehive.

'I have to go back inside and deal with the tearoom,' I told August. 'Shout if you need anything.'

He smiled and again his sarcasm tainted his tone. 'No, everything's fine. I'll just sit here and enjoy my afternoon tea.' He shrugged his broad shoulders. 'How bad could it be?'

A few spits of rain hit my face as I headed back inside. I glanced up at the blue sky. Dark clouds scurried along the skyline, shading out the blue.

Within minutes it was raining. Not just raining. Pouring down. Spring rain often arrived without warning even when the day had started bright and sunny.

'August's going to be really mad at me,' I confided to Kevin.

'I heard that he's got a head for heights, that he shimmied along a high ledge and climbed in a bedroom window,' said Kevin.

'Yes, he did,' I said, feeling a surge of enthusiasm. 'There's a metal ladder that runs from the kitchen upstairs in my flat down the side of the premises. He could climb up that and get out of the rain.'

Kevin nodded. 'I'll look after the customers.'

I ran upstairs to the flat, opened one of the kitchen windows and peered down at August. He'd taken his long coat off and was using it to shield himself from the downpour.

'August,' I shouted. 'Climb up the ladder. I'll help you in the kitchen window.'

He gazed up at me, and then threw his coat up. I managed to catch it.

'Be careful. The metal rungs will be wet with the rain,' I warned him.

But August could climb like a spider and soon his fabulous turquoise eyes were gazing straight at me as he peered over the ledge of the kitchen window. My stomach tightened when he looked at me. What a gorgeous man he was. Angry, but gorgeous.

I stepped back while he hauled himself inside, tumbling on to the floor, soaked to the skin but otherwise fine.

His cream shirt and dark trousers clung to every contour of his well–muscled physique. When he stood up, the fabric of his shirt had become soaked and sheer, giving me an eyeful of what was underneath. August's chest was strong and lean and his broad shoulders dripped water on to my kitchen floor. I didn't care. The view was worth it. Shame on me.

Then I noticed how his wet trousers clung to the athletic muscles of his long thighs. Oh yes, definitely shame on me for what I was thinking.

He gazed at me and I wondered what he was thinking. Probably that he could throttle me for the trouble I'd caused him.

'The bedroom and bathroom are through there,' I said. 'You can take your clothes off and dry them on the radiators. There are towels in the bathroom to cover your...particulars.'

He almost laughed and I felt the colour burn across my cheeks.

'What I meant was, you don't have to be naked. No...what I really meant was...you're welcome to get dried off before you drive home. Or you can just go as you are.' I cleared my throat and could've kicked myself for sounding so silly. It was obvious from my reaction that his manly physique, all six foot plus of it, had a desirable effect on me. I squirmed with embarrassment but tried to pretend that I was quite unaffected.

His lips formed into a sexy grin. Damn him.

He pushed his wet blond hair back from his face. His cheekbones had a sculptured quality as did his jaw. Up close I could see a few tiny scars on his face. Nothing very noticeable, perhaps highlighted by the rain that ran down the handsome contours that I wished my fingers could trace instead.

'You are trouble, Hazel. I should have known not to come here today.'

'Well, it's Saturday. Obviously the tearoom would be busy on a Saturday afternoon. You should've popped round for the hive at a quieter time.'

He nodded. 'I should have, but...I had a ridiculous notion...'

He looked down and tugged the fabric of his shirt from his muscled torso, shaking some of the rain from it.

'What notion?'

He shrugged his broad shoulders. 'I thought if I kept away, I'd stop thinking about you.'

My eyes widened as he gazed at me.

'I haven't been able to get you out of my thoughts since I met you, Hazel.'

My heart rate increased and I wasn't sure what to say.

'So I gave in and came round to get the hive — with an ulterior motive...to ask you to have dinner with me tonight. I thought that even a busy, trouble–making woman like you wouldn't work on a Saturday evening. And perhaps we could have dinner together at my house.'

'At your house?' the words burst from my lips. There was something so exciting, so intimate in his invitation.

'But of course now that we've been arguing I suppose that's out of the question,' he said.

'Well, it depends,' I told him.

Those turquoise eyes shot a surge of sensuality right through mine. 'It depends on what?'

'On whether I can use your front door. I'd rather not have to shimmy along any ledges or break–in.'

From the pocket of his trousers he brought out his keys. The key ring sparkled under the kitchen lights. 'No climbing required.'

I smiled and nodded.

'Does that mean we have a date?' he said.

'I guess it does,' I replied.

'I'll come back and pick you up at eight.'

He picked up his coat and headed downstairs. I followed him. A few customers watched the soaking wet, tall and handsome beemaster get into his car and drive off.

'Is he mad at you?' Elspeth said to me.

'Ask me on Monday. We're having dinner tonight — at his house.'

CHAPTER SIX

The Sparkly Sequin Dress

I ran around my flat like a woman possessed. It was 6:45pm. I'd showered, washed and dried my hair, put my makeup on and was in the process of rummaging through the uninspiring contents of my wardrobe for something suitable to wear for dinner with August. He wasn't due until eight but I hadn't been on a date in years and was well out of practice.

I held up a little black dress. Always a safe option but my pale complexion needed some oomph. I looked worn out and tired. I needed something that would perk me up, though every time I thought about August and how his wet clothes clung to every manly contour of his physique I felt myself flush. Maybe I wouldn't need any blusher after all.

I flung the black dress aside and delved deeper into the archives of a life of practicality with my ex. He didn't like parties or dancing. He preferred going to the cinema or staying at home and watching the television. This had resulted in my clothes becoming a washed–out version of my former self. There had been a time, back in the day, when I quite enjoyed getting dressed up and having a night out.

I pulled out several coat hangers full of drab garments. Where had I gone?

And then I saw something sparkle underneath a coat on one of the hangers at the back of the wardrobe. My heart jolted. Did I still have that sparkly red dress? I hadn't seen it in about two years. I'd bought it on impulse and against my ex's objections that there would never be any occasion when it would be suitable. It had never been worn, just gazed at sometimes, like looking at a life that I would never have. But there it was, hidden underneath a coat, enticing me to try it on.

I knew it would still fit because I hadn't changed in size. In fact, with all the hassle of the past few months I'd lost around ten pounds.

I stepped into the dress which was slightly stretchy and hugged my figure in all its sparkly red brilliance. It was cocktail length and not too low cut, but it really was a dazzler. I tried on a pair of dark gold heels. The height of the shoes changed my posture and now the dress was starting to look like it belonged to me, or I belonged to it. Probably the latter. This was the type of dress that wore you.

It was totally unsuitable for dinner with August but it cheered me up that I'd kept it. Then I saw a dark floral top that always made me feel okay. I was thinking of wearing it with a nice pair of black trousers when the doorbell rang.

I ran downstairs wearing the red dress. There was no time to take it off. I thought perhaps it would be Elspeth. I noticed she'd forgotten her sewing bag or maybe she'd intended leaving it under one of the sewing machine tables.

My stomach knotted when I saw that it wasn't Elspeth. It was August. He wore a dark suit, shirt and tie — and an expression that I translated as — what the hell is she wearing?

I opened the door and went to explain. And to ask what he was doing here so early. He wasn't due until eight. It wasn't even seven o'clock.

'Wow!' he said stepping slowly into the tearoom.

'I was trying on different outfits and —'

'You look sensational.'

I don't even think he heard a word I said as I explained about why I was wearing the equivalent of a firecracker. 'You said you'd be here at eight.'

'Yes, but I thought I'd pop round early,' he said. He hadn't taken his eyes off me. 'I never thought you'd look so...so...'

I held my breath. So flamboyant? Ridiculous (my ex's description).

He walked right up to me and his turquoise gaze nailed me to the spot. 'So sparkly and dazzling. Wow. Just wow, Hazel.'

So that was me stuck with the red dress for the evening. After his reaction I couldn't skulk upstairs and change into the dark top and nice trousers I'd have worn if he'd arrived later.

'Wait until they see you,' he added.

'They?'

'Yes, there's a change of plan. I'd intended having dinner at my house, but I've been invited to a party, a dinner dance type of function, in one of the hotels in the city.' He eyed me again. 'You're certainly dressed for the occasion.'

'A dinner dance?'

45

'Associates, people I do business with are having the party and they phoned to ask if I was free this evening. I said yes. I thought you'd like to go with me. Far more exciting than having me rustle up dinner for us.'

'Dinner with you sounded great.'

He smiled at me and I melted. 'I'll make dinner for us another night.' He clasped my hand. 'But tonight I think we should go to the party.'

'I'll get my bag and my coat,' I said.

He waited downstairs in the tearoom while I ran upstairs to the flat. I put on the black velvet coat that had been covering the dress and grabbed my bag. I saw myself in the wardrobe mirror. My hair was smooth and silky around the shoulders of the dark coat. Was I really going to do this? Go to a dinner dance with August on a whim?

'Are you ready?' August called to me.

'Yes.' I wrapped my coat around me like a shield and headed out into the night with the beemaster.

We drove through the city centre and August suggested we stop off at a lounge bar for a drink because we were early. The party didn't start for another hour.

The main bar was jumping with people so we headed through to the cocktail lounge. It was reasonably busy but we managed to get a table near the bar and sat down. I took my coat off and put it over the back of my chair.

'What can I get you?' a member of staff asked hardly looking at us. And then he said, 'Hazel, what are you doing here? And what are you wearing?' He held his hand up as if to shield himself from the dazzling sequins.

I gasped. 'Kevin.'

Kevin glared at August. 'Oh it's you. The beehive master.'

'Beemaster,' I said. 'August's a beemaster.' Then I said to August, 'I've put the hive back in the garden. The locksmith squirted some oil on the gate locks and they work fine now.'

'It's a shame you got soaked to the skin, isn't it?' Kevin said to him.

I shot Kevin a look.

46

'So, what can I get for you?' said Kevin, shifting into cocktail–making mode and forcing a smile at August.

'I'm driving so I'd like a non–alcoholic cocktail,' said August. 'What would you recommend?'

'A glass of lemonade,' said Kevin.

'I'd like a glass of lemonade,' I said. 'I could do with something refreshing.'

August nodded though I doubt this was what he had in mind when he stopped off at the bar.

Kevin went away and came back with our drinks in minutes.

August went to pay for them.

Kevin put his hand up. 'They're on me. Enjoy.' He walked away and then came back and said to me. 'You do realise that you're wearing a dress that can be seen from here to Kirkcaldy.'

I laughed. 'August won't lose me in the dark then will he?'

Kevin flicked a look at August and then whispered to me, 'I think he's mesmerised by the sequins.' He made his eyes swivel. 'I think they're going for me as well.'

Then he left us and went back behind the busy bar.

I looked around. We were probably the only two people in the cocktail lounge drinking lemonade. Not that anyone would know because the glasses Kevin served the drinks in were made from coloured glass and he'd decorated them with every type of fruit from strawberries to pineapples. Mine even had a cocktail cherry in it.

'I don't think Kevin likes me,' August remarked.

'I haven't known him long but I think he's taken it upon himself to look out for my interests.'

'Perhaps he fancies you and would like to ask you out. I wouldn't blame him, especially when you're wearing that dress.'

'I really didn't intend wearing this. I was trying it on when you arrived early. Otherwise I'd be sitting here in more subdued clothes.'

August sipped his drink. 'I'm glad I was early then.'

We chatted about my day at the tearoom, the wedding cake chaos, finished our drinks and then headed to the party. Kevin was serving customers and didn't see us leave.

August parked in the hotel car park and escorted me into the function room where the party was being held. Around a hundred guests had already arrived and the dinner tables around the dance floor were filled with well–dressed people. Everyone was dressed rather sedate. Very classy. Nothing ostentatious. The guests, August explained, were mainly business people and most of the ladies wore black or neutral coloured dresses.

'I feel they're staring at me,' I whispered to August as we were seated at one of the tables where another four guests were due to arrive.

'It's because you're stunning,' said August, smiling at me.

No, it's because you can see my dress from here to Kirkcaldy.

'What type of business is it you do with these people?' I asked August.

'Sometimes it's associated with the beekeeping, supplying them with honey or giving lecturers. Mainly it's to do with property. My grandfather left me a considerable amount of property and that's where I get my main income from. It allows me to continue with the beekeeping work and if the honey yield is low one year then I can supplement it with the income from my other business, my property work.'

I smiled at him. He looked really handsome sitting there at the table in his expensive dinner suit. His blond hair was sleeked back, tamed — but was August? For all his talk about property dealings there was an underlying adventurous streak in him that appealed to me in all sorts of exquisitely wicked ways.

'You really are a busy bee,' I said to August.

'He certainly is,' a man said, approaching our table and speaking in a confident voice.

I looked up to see a dark–haired man smiling down at me and eyeing my dress. He was tall and handsome and of a similar age to August. The look on the beemaster's face showed that they knew each other quite well.

'Good evening,' the man said to me and held out his hand. 'I'm Tavish and you're ravishing.' He kissed my hand when I reached out to shake his hand.

The gesture made August's shoulders tense. 'Her name is Hazel and she's with me.'

The man frowned and his lovely blue eyes looked at me. 'What are you doing with the beemaster? Don't you know he's only interested in bees? You're the most beautiful young lady August has ever brought to one of our events. He usually turns up with whatshername. That dour woman — Charliss.' He said to August, 'Are you still dating her?'

'We've never dated,' August told him.

The man's blue eyes flicked a look of disbelief and then he smiled at me. 'I hope you'll dance with me later, after the meal. I'm sure August will allow you to spare one dance for me.'

I nodded politely, sensing that trouble was brewing between the two of them. Tavish had deliberately approached us to get August's hackles up. And it had worked.

The other four guests arrived at our table and Tavish went back to his.

'I apologise for Tavish. We've been rivals, sometimes friendly rivals, sometimes not, for a long time.'

I was curious about his relationship with Charliss. 'He seems to think that you and Charliss are, or were, a couple.'

'No, we've never dated. Charliss helps out sometimes, freelance, with my business.' He paused and then confided, 'She'd like us to be more but I'm not interested in her like that.'

Tavish had wanted to create doubt in my mind about August and he had. The last thing I needed was another two–timing boyfriend. On the plus side, August didn't resemble a garden gnome. Quite the opposite. But perhaps his handsome looks were hiding a sneaky character?

Our dinner was served and by the fourth course one of the women at our table deemed to acknowledge me. She was in her early forties and wearing a black dress and jacket. The only sparkle was the mischief in her eyes.

'How very bold of you to wear a dress like that,' she said, smiling at me. 'I don't think I'd ever have the nerve to wear a dress like that in public.'

Don't let her upset you. Do not. I ignored her comment and ate my trifle.

There was a lull at the table as everyone waited on my response. I continued to eat my pudding.

'What is it you do for a living?' one of the other men asked, trying to sound polite and engage me in conversation.

'I bake scones, bread and cakes,' I said.

'Oh, you work for a bakery,' he said.

I don't think he was being deliberately awkward but the atmosphere at the table was not friendly.

I shook my head. 'No, I own a tearoom and bakery in Glasgow.'

Several sets of eyes perked up. What? Didn't they expect that I owned a business just because I was dressed like a firecracker?

'Hazel has recently opened a new vintage tearoom and bakery,' August elaborated. 'She bakes traditional cakes and it was Hazel who made the beehive cake for my recent promotion.'

The nasty cow swallowed any further comments about my dress, but I thought I'd ask her a question.

'So what is it you do for a living?' I said to her.

She fidgeted in her seat and then forced a smile. 'I'm married. I don't actually work.'

Any hope of a friendly social atmosphere at the table disappeared.

A waiter topped up our glasses with champagne. August kept to soft drinks but I decided to indulge a little. 'I don't really drink champagne,' I whispered to August. 'I rarely drink anything other than tea.'

Although I had every intention of having one glass, okay, two glasses of champagne, I lost count and felt a little bit frisky and naughty and...wild.

'Do not let me drink any more champagne,' I said to August. 'I've had two glasses or four too many already.'

August smiled at me. 'Well, don't start dancing on the tables. Even though I'd pay to see that.'

'I'd definitely pay to see that,' Tavish said over my shoulder.

August's smile vanished and he glared at Tavish.

Tavish held his hand out to me. 'You promised me a dance and I'm here to collect it.' He looked at August. 'You don't mind, do you? One dance with your lovely young lady.'

August gave him a grudging smile.

I let Tavish escort me on to the dance floor. Lots of couples were up dancing. Nothing wild, all very classy. Tavish held me in his arms and we began to waltz slowly around the floor. All was okay for about two minutes and then the music changed to a lively Scottish reel.

This was when the party really got going. Dinner and plenty of drink had been consumed. Even those who were wearing drab clothes were ready to let their hair down for some Scottish dancing.

I went to leave the floor. Tavish pulled me back.

'Come on, Hazel. Let's give that dress of yours a whirl. You'll dazzle them all.'

'I don't think that's a good idea,' I said.

'Nonsense. That's what parties are for — to dance and enjoy ourselves and for a little bit of scandal.'

And so Tavish whirled me around the dance floor. I managed to keep up with him. I liked reels and traditional dancing and the champagne had encouraged me to drop my usual reserve. Or perhaps deep down this really was me, the wild little brunette that my ex had tried to tame. He'd succeeded quite well. But now I was in the mood to let rip with a few moves that even Tavish wasn't ready for.

We left the party earlier than planned. August put me in the car and we drove off from the hotel. His shirt was torn and he looked like he'd been in a tussle.

I could hear from his breathing that he was angry. With me, with Tavish and with himself.

'I didn't start the fight,' I said, cutting through the thick atmosphere in the car. 'There's no way I'm taking all the blame for what happened. You shouldn't have punched Tavish.'

'He was feeling your arse on the dance floor.'

'I slapped his jaw for him and stepped away. You didn't need to lunge at him with your fists flailing.'

'He'd been spoiling for a fight all night so I gave him one.'

'Do you think his nose will be okay?'

'Yes, it might even be an improvement. Besides, he should keep his ruddy nose out of my business and out of my personal life. He had no right to flirt with you.'

'It was quite impressive how you dived across the table. You didn't even disturb the table cloth.'

There was silence again as we drove through the city.

'I wish I'd stuck to my original plan and had dinner at my house,' he said, sounding upset with himself.

'Another time,' I said.

51

'You still want to see me again, even after the fiasco this evening?'

'Yes, it was just totally embarrassing and a huge punch–up in the middle of the dance floor in front of a load of posh business people who were shocked at how you attacked Tavish.' I tried to make light of it. Was that a hint of a smile on those sexy lips of his?

'Quite a few of them saw your knickers.'

'No,' I said. 'The sequins dazzled them. They wouldn't have seen anything except those.'

'Ah, so there was method in you wearing that dress. I thought maybe you'd worn it to make you irresistible.' He grinned at me. 'And if so, let me tell you that it worked.'

'I'd better not ask you in for a coffee,' I said as we pulled up outside the tearoom.

'No. I couldn't promise not to kiss you and who knows where that would lead. But I do insist on seeing you safely inside.' He got out of the car and helped me open the front door.

I wasn't tipsy. I'd had no more champagne. But I was feeling quite giddy from all the excitement of the evening and from the way August was gazing at me. Those eyes of his made me want to grab him, kiss him and damn the consequences. But I didn't. I went inside the tearoom and only wobbled because my high heels snagged on the flooring. August steadied me.

'I'm fine,' I assured him. 'Thanks for a wild time.'

He looked at me and any anger appeared to have gone. 'Are you always so much trouble, Hazel, or will we blame the dress?'

'You want me to lie?' I said.

He shook his head. 'No, I'd rather we were always honest with each other.'

I thought he was going to leave without another word. And I was right, but he didn't leave without kissing me.

He held me in his arms, squeezed me tight and kissed me with raw passion and a feeling that he really did care about me. I kissed him, wishing it could last for longer but knowing he was right — it would only lead to other things and I wasn't the type to leap into bed so early in a relationship. August's shirt was torn, but he wouldn't lose any buttons from it by my hands tonight, even though I was tempted.

He drove off and I locked up the tearoom. It still had some of the warmth from earlier. I flicked the lamp off and noticed the sparkly key ring on the counter.

Hopefully August wouldn't blame me when he had to climb in through his bedroom window again. It wasn't my fault he'd forgotten his keys. He'd put them down to steady me and left them lying on the counter.

No, it definitely wasn't my fault I told myself and went upstairs to bed.

Tomorrow was Sunday. I planned to get up early and make a start on the garden, tackling the weeds and seeing what I could do with the old shed.

CHAPTER SEVEN

Shed in the City

I was up early to tackle the garden and enjoy the gorgeous spring day. I'd dressed in jeans and a jumper and opened up the patio doors to let the fresh air waft into the tearoom while I worked in the garden.

The sky was a bright blue. The light breeze was mild and although I worked hard I felt any tensions from the previous night ease from my shoulders. It felt satisfying to pull out the weeds and clip the spindly branches off the trees and bushes. The harsh winter had dried everything to a crisp and it was a lot easier to tidy up than I'd anticipated. The weeds pulled free of the soil without too much effort and soon I'd cleared the bulk of them and filled three rubbish bags full of the garden debris.

A few spring flowers had somehow fought through and when I pulled the weeds aside yellow and lilac crocus were growing near the one of the trees.

I kicked the dirt from my boots and went inside to make a cup of tea in the tearoom kitchen. It was around 10:00am and I noticed two large builders vans pulling up outside. Bert was in the first one along with another workman in the passenger seat. They got out and Bert came to the door. Another two men opened the rear doors of the second van.

'Morning, Hazel,' Bert said, sounding chirpy. He was all smiles as he approached me. 'I've got a wee pressie for you.'

I couldn't imagine what it was. 'A present for me? I thought you'd be relaxing after the wedding.'

He shook his head. 'Shevonne's away to Spain for her honeymoon and Bridie's making my Sunday dinner for later. But I wanted to give you something in appreciation for what you did. Sorting the wedding cake, and running round like a peerie on that pink bike of yours through the traffic to help us...well...things like that don't go unrewarded, not in my world.'

'I wasn't looking for anything, Bert.'

'I know that, and that's what makes it all the more important. You did it out of the kindness of your heart. You certainly saved my daughter's wedding reception, her special day, from going to shit — in more ways than one,' he added with a smile.

The other men started to unload long pieces of wood — and what looked like a roof.

I stood aside as they carried them through the tearoom and out into the garden as I spoke to Bert.

Bert smiled proudly. 'That shed you've got in the garden is hanging together by a few nails, so I've brought you a new one.'

My voice perked up. 'A new shed?'

Bert nodded as more parts of the shed were carried in carefully through the tearoom without causing any mess. Then the workmen brought their tools through and started to work like bees in the garden. They tore the old shed down in minutes.

'Is there a side entrance we can trail the rubbish through instead of the tearoom?' said Bert.

'Yes, I'll open the side gates.' I hurried to open them and then joined Bert outside on the patio as he organised the assembling of the new shed.

'This is far too generous, Bert. You didn't need to do this.'

'Yes I did, Hazel. I know I look like just a builder, but I'm what they call fairly well off.' He gave me a wink. 'My building company makes sheds and this is one of our new prototypes. It's quite spacious, already treated to deal with the weather but you can paint it if you want. The interior walls are lined with cream panelling that makes it look like a wee house when it's finished. And you can repaint it if you prefer another colour.' He pulled out a sketch of the interior and a picture of the finished shed. 'What do you think? A stoater isn't it?'

'It's fantastic.'

'I'm glad you like it. Bridie and I thought you would. We'll rig it up with full power for electricity and so forth. You can even use it as an extension of the tearoom.'

'I don't know how to thank you,' I said, feeling quite teary and overcome.

Bert put a hand on my shoulder. 'You're more than welcome, hen. My Shevonne's got happy memories of her wedding day reception because of you. She was fair upset about that cake. The cake was a big deal to her. Besides, this will let folk see the new shed in all it's finery.'

I made tea and cakes for Bert and the workmen who scoffed the lot while continuing to assemble the shed.

It looked amazing. I stood at the patio and watched my garden being transformed. The timing was perfect because I'd already cleared most of the weeds. Anything that was left was ripped up and flung in the workmen's bags and carried out to their vans. They cleared the lot, leaving the shed standing in pride of place.

By mid–day everything was assembled and the power installed.

I made everyone lunch — soup, sandwiches, scones, cake and gallons of tea and coffee. I felt so excited about the shed. I loved it. Loved it. It fitted into the garden setting with its traditional shed design. Bert screwed in hooks so that I could put hanging baskets of flowers on the outside, similar to the frontage of the tearoom. He'd thought of everything.

'Would you like a wooden counter along that wall?' Bert offered. 'We've got various worktops from the kitchens we do up. And folding tables that I brought along. We'll kit it out for you with shelves while we're here. I brought plenty of stuff. Bridie suggested the table tops.'

'Eh, yes, that would be brilliant,' I said.

The weather had remained lovely throughout the day and I had a smile on my face for most of the time. A new shed! I couldn't believe it. It would be so handy. By late afternoon the work was finished.

'Okay, Hazel,' Bert called to me. 'Come and step over the threshold of your new shed in the city.'

'I think that's what I'll call it,' I said, stepping inside the beautiful structure. 'Oh, it's like a wee house. Or rather, a big wee house.' There were shelves, a corner cabinet, four folding tables, a counter and room to move around and breathe. 'What a fantastic design, Bert. I don't know how to thank you.'

Bert smiled. 'This is me thanking you, Hazel. I wish you all the luck in the world with your business. We'll be popping in regularly for cakes, so you haven't seen the last of us. If there are any other wee jobs you need sorted, more shelves or whatever, give me a shout. And don't worry about height restrictions for the shed. It's deceiving. Your old shed was tall and pointy and the new one is actually the same height only wider and more spacious.'

Bert and the workmen packed up their things and left me to enjoy my new shed. They'd put August's hive aside and helped arrange my solar lights around the garden.

I don't know how long I stood there admiring the shed, pottering around the garden and wondering what August, Kevin, Elspeth and the customers would think when they arrived on Monday morning to see the garden totally transformed.

I smiled to myself and drank a cup of tea in the doorway of the shed. Yes, I thought to myself. This shed in the city had the potential to be a tearoom. No...a tea shop. A little tea shop in the garden. My lease agreement allowed for food and beverages to be served outside in the garden. I couldn't wait to get it up and running.

And so I didn't.

I drove to a nearby gardening shop and bought some hanging baskets pre–filled with spring flowers — miniature daffodils, crocus and bluebells, garden tubs planted with flowers and several little tea lanterns for the tables in the tea shop. They were a real bargain at only a few pounds for the lanterns and I thought their vintage look would suit the decor.

I hung the baskets up outside the shed and put the spare one at the front of the tearoom. The tubs of flowers added a touch of spring to the entrance of the shed and under the windows. I loved that there were windows on the sides of the shed and one beside the door because as the light changed during the day the shed would always have plenty of daylight shining in. It gave a cheerful ambiance to the interior, as did the tea lanterns.

I made a tomato and lettuce sandwich for my dinner. Kevin wouldn't have approved, but I was so excited and fired up with energy to create the tea shop ready for the next morning. Okay, so I didn't have everything I needed, but I had enough to make it look fine.

The day had faded into a mild twilight of lilac and amber and the solar lights were starting to flicker ready to illuminate the shed as the early evening approached.

I ran up and down to the flat, using items from my own belongings to add little touches such as ceramic teapots and a vase of flowers to the tea shop. I had two old–fashioned tea caddies that I'd had for years and put them up on one of the shelves. I used a vintage lamp with a fringed shade and plugged it into one of the power points that Bert had installed. It lit up the counter with a soft, warm glow. I put Bert's business card, that he'd given to me the first day he'd come into the tearoom, into a tiny antique frame that had once held a floral picture. Then I hung the framed card near the inside of the door so that if anyone asked who made the shed I could point to the card and they could contact Bert.

I remembered that there was a spare chalkboard stand tucked into the tearoom pantry cupboard so I scrubbed it and sat it beside the tea shop counter. I hoovered a large rug that was in my living room and put it down in the shed to give a feeling of homely comfort.

The sky was filled with stars by the time I'd finished working in the shed. The lights from the city sparkled all around the garden. And right in the middle of it the shed glowed in the darkness like a beacon of hope.

This would work, I told myself, having another cup of tea before going upstairs to get some sleep. Shed in the city would open on Monday morning. Another fresh start for me.

It was 11:00pm when I realised I hadn't heard a peep from August. He hadn't even come back for his house keys. I'd been so caught up in the shed that the whole day had slipped by without remembering about his keys. Or perhaps he'd had another set cut.

When the doorbell rang I peered out the living room window and saw him standing on the street gazing up at me. I grabbed his keys and ran down to give them to him — not thinking that my comfy leggings, jumper and ridiculously fluffy slippers would be such a contrast to my previous night's outfit. My hair was pulled up in a ponytail and my face was scrubbed clean of make up. But all the activity and a day outdoors had given me a glow and I thought I looked less weary and pale.

I dangled the keys and smiled at him.

He stepped inside. He wore his long coat open and a soft granddad style top with the buttons undone at the neckline. It was the type of fabric that I wanted to snuggle against, or perhaps I just wanted to snuggle against August's broad chest.

He accepted the keys and kissed the tips of my fingers as he smiled at me. 'I didn't deliberately leave them. It wasn't an excuse to come back here.'

'I believe you.'

He took in what I was wearing. 'You look lovely.'

I laughed. 'No sequins tonight.'

His expression deepened. 'You don't need them, Hazel. You're lovely as you are.'

'I thought you liked the red dazzler,' I said, teasing him.

'I did, but I like you, Hazel.' He pulled me close and kissed me, wrapping me up in an embrace that made me forget everything except him.

He eventually let me go and cleared his throat. 'Sequins or fluffy slippers — how am I ever going to resist you?'

I didn't want him to resist me, and yet deep down we were both holding back from taking things further so fast. August was concerned about not having time for a proper relationship. After the trouble with my ex I was also wary of getting involved with someone else, especially when I'd just started up the business. I needed to build up the tearoom and now the tea shop.

'Would you like to be the first to see something special?' I said. I heard the excitement in my voice as I looked at him.

'I'm up for that.'

I led him to the back of the tearoom. 'Close your eyes and don't peek until I tell you.'

'Okay.'

I opened the patio doors and left August standing there while I lit the tea lanterns and flicked on the vintage lamp inside the shed.

'You can look now,' I called to him.

August opened his eyes and blinked as if he couldn't believe what was in the garden.

'Do you like it?'

'It's spectacular. How did you manage to get it...I mean, last night the old shed was there and now...'

I explained about Bert.

August came out and looked around the shed, admiring the handiwork before stepping inside and gazing at the interior.

'I'm going to use it as a tea shop,' I told him.

'A tea shop?'

'Yes, like the tearoom. I'll sell packets of tea and I'll serve afternoon teas out here. Teas with a vintage touch and traditional baking — Victoria sponges, scones with cream and jam, fairy cakes and ice cream.'

'I love it!' He ran his hands along the smooth edges of the wooden counter and felt the finish on the door lintel. Bert and his men had even set the shed on sleepers to prevent the floor becoming damp and had added all sorts of little touches that made the craftsmanship stand out.

August nodded and wandered around the shed. 'Do you think Bert would make a shed like this for me? I'd pay the going rate of course. I'm not looking for any bargains or favours.'

'I'm sure he would.' I pointed to the card I'd hung up. 'There's his business card. I framed it.'

August tapped Bert's telephone number into his mobile. 'I'll call him tomorrow. I've been working with the bees from my old shed and the roof was almost blown off during the winter storms. This would be ideal. In fact, I could do with two of them. One for up at the house and the other for my base on the outskirts of the city.'

From what August had been telling me about his income from the property he owned I reckoned he could easily afford to buy two sheds from Bert.

I put the lights off in the shed and we stepped out into the garden. The cool night air had a sense of new beginnings to it.

'You can take the beehive with you if you want.' I pointed to it at the other side of the patio.

August looked at it thoughtfully. 'Do you think that Bert could build me some new beehives, like the old one?'

'Bert's got a building business. I'm sure he could. He seems to be able to do various types of work.'

'Can I leave the beehive here for a little longer?'

'Yes.'

He lifted it up and put it back near its original setting opposite the shed. Somehow it completed the garden.

'It looks like it belongs here,' I said.

'It does, doesn't it?' he agreed. He stepped closer to me, gazing down at me. His eyes were brimming with warmth and passion. 'Hopefully I do too, but we'll take things slowly. As you said last night, you're not ready to get involved yet, but I've got a feeling that we could have a future together.'

I nodded up at him.

He smiled and kissed the tip of my nose.

'Get some sleep, Hazel. You've worked hard today. I'll call Bert tomorrow and let you know what he says.'

I locked up after August left and took one last look at the shed before going to bed. I couldn't wait for the morning. So many plans were running through my mind — a menu for the tea shop, other things I'd need such as vintage cake stands and flowery teacups with mismatched saucers, tea strainers and napkins. And a tea shop sign for the front of the shed. Kevin would help me, and at the rate he worked we'd have everything ready by Wednesday.

I slept sound from all the fresh air and excitement. When my alarm went off I jumped out of bed, into the shower and got the day started downstairs in the tearoom kitchen.

A light shimmer of frost across the grass in the garden hinted that another lovely day of mild spring weather was due. Perfect for anyone wanting to see the new tea shop. I couldn't wait to see Kevin's reaction when he arrived. I knew I'd be in for a grilling as well about the red sequin dress. But it didn't matter. I'd brush over the altercation and fisticuffs between August and Tavish.

I let Kevin in while the cakes and scones were in the ovens.

He shrugged his jacket off and the first thing he noticed was the shed. The sun streamed in through the patio doors and the shed shone in the early morning sunlight.

'What the...?' He ran over to peer outside.

I hurried after him and opened the doors.

'How did you get this?'

I told him all about Bert and the workmen.

I opened the shed door and he was even more impressed when he saw how lovely it was inside. 'Did you do this?'

'Some of it. But Bert and his men put up the shelves, the counter, all the fixtures and fittings. I decorated it with plants and teapots and lights. I thought perhaps you'd like to help me get it ready for opening to customers. We could have it ready by —'

'Tuesday.'

61

Yes, Kevin was quick off the mark. No complaints from me whatsoever.

'I know where we can get an ice cream making machine. One of the restaurants I used to work for is buying new equipment. There's nothing wrong with the old stuff. In fact, the old–fashioned look of it will suit the shed. I'll phone them and see what they want for it. It shouldn't cost much and I'm always doing them favours.'

So Kevin was on a mission to collect other items for the tea shop, leaving me to get the day going at the tearoom.

Elspeth arrived and she was equally surprised. She offered to make table cloths and other items from the fabric stash I had for customers to use at the sewing tables. I'd brought down a whole lot of material remnants from my flat that I knew I wouldn't have time to sew and hoped it would encourage other customers to have a go at sewing.

'I'll phone my Auntie Janetta and the ladies. They'll love to make stuff. It's always great to have a reason for making pretty items and seeing them put to use.' Elspeth sounded enthusiastic and judging by the phone call to Janetta, the shed was about to be decorated to the max.

I used two jars of August's honey, both different flavours, to make honey cakes. While helping Elspeth serve customers, including a few police officers who had made the tearoom a regular stopover, I created fondant bees to put on the cakes. I sliced the honey cakes into wedges, each one with at least one bumblebee.

August phoned me. 'Bert's coming over to my house to size up the garden for the new shed. And I asked him about making wooden beehives. He says it's no problem. He's going to drop by the tearoom and take measurements of the old hive if that's okay.'

'Yes, that's fine. I'm pleased you're going to do business with him.'

'I'm working this evening, but I'll call you tomorrow,' said August. 'We'll make a date for you to come over to my house for dinner.'

With everything bubbling away I realised that things were going well — and I hadn't caused any trouble for at least twenty–four hours. Yay!

CHAPTER EIGHT

Butterfly Cake and Intrigue

Doyle arrived after lunch and got a tour of the shed from Elspeth.

'Has Doyle asked her out yet?' Kevin said to me, topping up the milk jugs with fresh milk and cream while I added butterfly cakes, tattie scones, sugar buns, Empire biscuits and Bakewell tarts to the cake stands.

We watched Doyle and Elspeth flirt with each other. She wanted to try on his policeman's hat but he wouldn't let her.

'No, I think he's a bit like August. Wary of getting involved.'

'That's daft,' said Kevin. 'They obviously fancy each other — as do you and August, though I've still to hear your explanation for dressing up like a distress beacon.'

'It's a long story.'

'You can tell me while we're clearing up later. I want all the details.'

I laughed at him. 'You sound like a sweetie wife.'

'I'm just looking out for you, Hazel. There's something about August that sets my alarm bells clanging.'

'I think August is okay.'

Kevin's bright blue eyes gazed down at me. 'But you're not totally sure, are you?'

I brushed his comment aside and nudged him when I saw Doyle and Elspeth heading back inside.

'I'm going to come straight out and ask Doyle,' said Kevin.

'No, don't do that.' I pulled at the elbow of his shirt but Kevin made a beeline for Doyle while Elspeth came over to the counter to serve customers.

I tried to eavesdrop on Kevin and Doyle's conversation. I heard snippets.

'Have you not asked Elspeth out yet?' said Kevin.

Doyle squirmed in his policeman's sturdy boots. 'I know you're pals with Elspeth but is it any of your business sonny?'

Kevin was unperturbed. 'Sometimes it takes an interfering busybody like me to encourage two people who fancy each other to get together.'

Doyle's serious features broke into a smile.

'Why don't you ask Elspeth out on a date?'

Doyle sighed heavily. 'Because...'

The coffee machine decided to let off steam just as Doyle was revealing all. Damn it!

'But that's silly,' Kevin said in reply to Doyle's reason.

'Is it? How would you like it if the woman you were dating was only interested in you because you could bake cakes?'

Kevin shrugged. 'I'd be happy with that. It's what I do. I can bake anything. It's part of me, part of my life.'

'That's okay for you, but when you're at home with a girlfriend you can always pop through to the kitchen and mix up meringues or whatever the hell it is you do. But when I'm at home I'm out of my uniform and every woman I've ever been involved with has fancied me first and foremost because of the uniform. I've even heard Elspeth tell those lassies she's friends with when they're sewing that she loves a man in uniform.'

'So do a lot of women,' Kevin argued.

'Yes but I'd like a woman to love me for me, not because of the uniform or because I'm a police officer.'

'Then there's only one solution,' Kevin told him.

'What's that?'

'Start dropping by here in your plain clothes. Let Elspeth get a gander at you without your uniform on. If she's still smitten, then ask her out.'

I saw Doyle nod.

Had Kevin really talked Doyle into this? It seemed so.

Doyle gave me a friendly wave as he left the tearoom. I went over to Kevin. 'I heard the gist of what you said to Doyle. You shouldn't interfere with people's lives. I know from experience. It causes nothing but trouble.'

'No Hazel, that's just you. You'd cause trouble in an empty shed. When I stick my nose into people's business I usually make things work out for them.'

'Why is there one rule for me and a different rule for you, Kevin?'

'Because I'm jammy and you're not.'

'Can I have another slice of that honey cake with a bumblebee on it?' A customer called to us.

'I'll sort it,' said Kevin, picking up a cake server.

Kevin's friend dropped off the ice cream machine and a few other items later that afternoon.

I went to get some money.

'They don't want anything for them,' said Kevin. 'They were going to throw them away. The restaurant owners are loaded with money. This is nothing to them.'

I beamed with delight when I saw the ice cream machine. 'It looks in great condition.'

'Everything's been well looked after. And I know how to work it. I've made ice cream before, various flavours, but there's nothing like old–fashioned vanilla ice cream. It's perfect to go with cakes and scones as well as on its own or as a pokey–hat or a wafer. I'll give everything a clean later when you're telling me all the gossip about last night — and the punch–up.'

He knew?

'Don't look at me like that. Of course I know. August and Tavish had a fight in the hotel. I know some of the staff. There are no secrets in the bar and restaurant grapevine.' He tapped the side of his nose. 'So don't bother skirting around the issue. I know you caused the fight.'

'I didn't.'

'That dress of yours was asking for trouble. What the hell were you wearing that for? You looked like a showgirl — all jazzed up to go to a snooty party like that. It would be fine for a girls' glitzy night out but not for a staid dinner dance.'

'August arrived early.' I sounded exasperated.

'You should've asked him to wait ten minutes while you put something less daring on.'

'Maybe I wanted to be daring,' I said a bit louder than I intended.

'Let Hazel be daring if she wants to be,' one of the customers called over. 'And I'll have another Scottish fancy with pink icing if you've got one, Kevin.'

'Is that mince and tatties I smell cooking?' a customer commented as they came into the tearoom to buy soda scones and teacakes.

I sniffed. 'Yes...' I left Elspeth to serve the customers. It was nearly closing time, almost five o'clock. Most of the tables had cleared and only a few late customers were popping in to buy something for their Monday night tea before we shut the tearoom.

Kevin was washing up and cleaning the kitchen while Elspeth helped me serve at the counter and wipe down the tables.

I followed the savoury aroma through to the kitchen. Two small pots were simmering away on the cooker.

'Is that mince and tatties?' I said to Kevin. He was due to leave to work at the bar. What was he cooking these for? We didn't even sell stuff like this for customers.

'It is,' he said, scrubbing the baking trays. 'It's your dinner.'

'My dinner?'

He continued washing up while giving me a mild telling off. 'You don't eat right. I saw the sandwich crusts from last night's lavish dinner, so when I was out earlier I bought some mince, carrots, onions, potatoes and gravy. And I don't want the money for them. It didn't cost a lot.'

I went to take the lid off one of the pots. The food smelled delicious, and I had to admit that I was hungry.

'Don't take the lid off the pot,' Kevin told me. 'I'm steaming the tatties to make them all nice and fluffy. I'll mash them up with a knob of butter before I leave.'

I smiled at him. Kevin had made my dinner. I was looking forward to it. And I made a promise to myself to start making proper meals for myself.

'Thanks, Kevin,' I said to him and went back through to finish up in the tearoom.

As Elspeth was leaving she said to me, 'I keep meaning to ask you — what happened to your gnome? Was he released from police custody? Have you got him upstairs in your flat? I haven't seen him in the garden.'

Guilt shot through me. 'I eh...August wanted to borrow him for his eh...his beehives in his garden.'

Her face lit up as if this made sense to her. 'I'm sure August will look after your gnome and you'll get him back for the summer.'

I smiled at her and waved her off.

Kevin put his jacket on. I gave him a kiss on the cheek as he was leaving. He knew what it was for. My dinner was ready.

And so was the tea shop. I'd sorted out a menu and wrote it on the chalk board. *Traditional cakes, scones and baking served with morning and afternoon tea. Ice cream on request.*

Kevin said he'd whip up a batch of ice cream the next morning, and we'd invite customers from the tearoom to have their afternoon tea outside in the shed.

Janetta and the sewing ladies said they'd have some of the items finished by the morning. Elspeth would iron them and bring them in. They'd made floral curtains for the windows in the shed.

Bert had stopped by to measure the hive. He also took photographs. Apparently August had ordered a lot of new hives and Bert was pleased to make them for him. So all was well.

Hmmm...not quite. I was concerned about Doyle. What if Elspeth didn't fancy him out of uniform? I tried to imagine what he'd look like in plain clothes. I was so used to seeing him dressed as a police officer. The first time I'd met him I thought he was handsome but had the uniform added to his looks? If Elspeth was only seeing the uniform and not the man, would Doyle stop dropping by the tearoom if their romance fizzled out when he revealed his casual self?

I sat at the kitchen table and ate the mince and tatties that Kevin had made for me. He could bake anything, but he could also cook up a delicious dinner. This would put some meat on my bones.

I'd finished washing the dishes when the doorbell rang.

I saw a figure standing outside the door. The man smiled in at me, and that's when I realised who it was — Doyle.

Any worries that Elspeth wouldn't fancy the casual version of him were thrown aside.

'Doyle,' I said, staring at him. He wore jeans, a dark open–neck top and a black outdoors jacket that displayed the width of his broad shoulders to full effect. Casual but gorgeous.

'What do you think? Or more to the point. What do you think Elspeth will think?'

'I'd be prepared if I was you,' I warned him. 'She is going to flip — and so are the other women when they see you.'

He looked embarrassed. 'I'm on duty tonight but I thought I'd give this a test run past you. I thought I could rely on you telling me the truth. I'm off duty tomorrow.'

'Elspeth is working in the tearoom for most of the day. I won't tell her you're coming in. I'll let you surprise her.' And what a surprise she was going to get.

He left with more confidence than when he arrived. Elspeth had to fancy Doyle when she saw him dressed like that. She had to.

Before finishing up for the night, I baked some cakes, or used cakes that I had already made, for the opening of the tea shop. Those that I had included Dundee cake, marble cake, iced Madeira and walnut cake with coffee icing, cherry cake and Scottish whisky cake. I baked a lemon drizzle cake, strawberry chiffon cake, chocolate fudge cake, Victoria sponge, chocolate sponge, and a buttercream and vanilla cake. I had the dozen cakes ready to cut and assemble in the morning.

I planned to cut each cake into twelve slices and then rotate the slices so that each of the twelve cakes contained a dozen different slices of cake. I'd done this for a party the previous year and people loved the assorted cakes, each one looking like a finished cake.

I ordered more stock of flour and other bakery products online and before closing my laptop I checked my emails. There was one message — from Tavish.

I clicked on it and read the email aloud. 'Hazel, can we meet sometime? I'd like to talk to you about August. There are a few things you should know especially if you're considering dating him. I still think that he's involved with Charliss and I'm not the only one. Call me and we'll arrange to meet when it suits you. Tavish.'

I sat back in my chair and studied the message. I wondered how he'd got my private email address. Had August given it to him? Or someone else? And why was he determined to tell me about August? My first instinct was to phone August and tell him. I dialled his number but there was no reply. I didn't leave a message for him. It was too complicated to explain.

Any hint of suspicion I'd had on Sunday regarding August's relationship with Charliss had faded. Now the suspicions were back again. Then I remembered what Kevin had said, '*There's something about August that sets my alarm bells clanging.*' What if Kevin's instincts were correct? I'd been wrong about my ex. Was I about to make the same mistakes again — trusting a man who was leading a double life and involved with another woman?

I waited and tried August's mobile number again. His phone was switched off.

I looked at Tavish's email and then called him. He picked up on the second ring.

'It's Hazel. I got your email.'

'Are you at the tearoom?' said Tavish.

'Yes.'

'Can I come over?'

'Tonight? It's really late.' Then I reconsidered. 'Okay.'

'I'm on my way. Don't tell August, though I suppose he's busy with Charliss this evening.'

'He was working and he had a lecture tonight.'

'He cancelled the lecture.'

My hopes of trusting August fell again and I clicked the phone off.

I tidied myself, brushed my hair and went downstairs. I put the kettle on for tea.

Tavish drove up in a sleek sports car. I opened the tearoom door. He looked handsome in his suit but I didn't trust him.

'Would you like a cup of tea or coffee?'

'Coffee. Milk no sugar.'

I made a coffee for Tavish. I had a cup of tea.

We sat down at one of the tables in the tearoom.

He glanced out the patio doors. 'Is that the shed that August's having put in his garden?'

'You seem to know a lot about August's business.'

'That's because we're rivals. Always know what your competitors are up to.'

'Are you a beemaster?'

'No, I'm in the property business.'

'So that's where your rivalry comes from.'

He stirred his coffee. 'Sometimes, but that's business. Our paths have crossed on other matters. I was engaged two years ago and August stepped in and stole her away from me.'

'Maybe he didn't do it deliberately.'

'Oh yes he did,' said Tavish. 'He knows that women are taken in by his looks. He's handsome and he knows how to use it. He used it on her and she left me for him.'

'What happened to their relationship?'

'Nothing. They went out a few times and then he became too busy with his beekeeping and they spit up. We didn't get back together. She moved away and got on with her life.'

'You're obviously very bitter.'

'I think I've got a reason to be.'

We were quiet for a moment.

'I'll tell you straight, Tavish, I don't trust you. And if you've got some sort of feud going between you and August, I want no part of it.'

He drank his coffee and then stood up. 'Don't say I didn't warn you. August is involved with Charliss. You're just a fleeting interest.'

I opened the front door of the tearoom. 'Thanks for stopping by, Tavish, but don't make a habit of it.'

He smiled and walked out to his car, glancing back once to give me a triumphant wave as he drove off.

I had a feeling he'd achieved what he'd set out to do — to drive a wedge of doubt between August and me. Now I had to do what I'd always done — decide for myself. Make my own choices. I'd opened up the tearoom and bakery when others thought I'd never make it.

I drank my tea and gazed out the window at the city. Could I trust the beemaster? And should I tell him about my meeting with Tavish?

As I watched the traffic going past I phoned August and left a message for him. I told him the gist of what had happened and then hung up.

August had wanted us to be honest with each other, but I'd probably stirred up a hornet's nest for the beemaster.

CHAPTER NINE

Afternoon Tea at the Tea Shop

Kevin arrived at the tearoom carrying something behind his back. He seemed very pleased with himself.

'What have you got there?' I said, trying to peek behind him.

'I walked past the early morning markets and look what I found sitting at one of the stalls.' He grinned as he presented me with a garden gnome. 'It's the same as the one you let August borrow for his bees. You can put it out beside the shed. Once August gives you the other one back you'll have a set. You can put one on either side of the garden.' He sounded so pleased. My heart sank as I reluctantly told him the truth.

I showed him the dent on the gnome's bum. 'That's where I kicked his backside when I split up with my ex.'

'So it's the same gnome?'

I nodded.

Kevin burst out laughing. 'I heard you telling Elspeth that August borrowed the gnome. You sounded so disheartened,' he said between gasps of laughter.

'No, I was feeling guilty at telling her fibs. I didn't want to upset her. She'd been kind in bringing the gnome back. I didn't have the heart to tell her I'd tried to get rid of him. Doyle took him away again.'

'But somehow he was on sale at the market,' he said.

'Don't tell Elspeth.'

He shook his head. 'What are we going to do with the gnome?'

Before we could discuss this further, Elspeth arrived early. 'Oh you've got your gnome back. Is August done with him?'

Kevin had to hurry away because he couldn't stop laughing.

'Is Kevin okay?' she said.

'Yes, he's eh...he's just excited about us opening the tea shop. We've got a lot to do.'

'I'll help you.' She picked up the gnome. 'I'll put him out in the garden for you, Hazel. He'll look sweet beside the new shed.'

Kevin came back from wherever he'd been guffawing.

I whispered to him as we watched Elspeth sit the gnome at the front of the shed. 'There was nothing I could do.'

'We could raffle him off,' said Kevin, giggling.

He was joking but I thought it was a great idea. 'Yes, we could buy a book of raffle tickets from the grocery shop. We could give him away as a prize as part of the tea shop opening.'

'We'd need other prizes.'

'Cakes. We'll give away cakes, make it a proper promotion.'

'Cakes and a garden gnome?' Kevin smiled and shook his head. 'It sounds like a recipe for trouble.'

I baked cakes and scones galore while Kevin whisked up a load of vanilla ice cream.

As customers came in for tea we gave them a raffle ticket and entered them into the prize draw. I was amazed how enthusiastic people were about the raffle. It went down a treat. We told everyone we were having the raffle at three in the afternoon.

'I wonder who will win the gnome?' Kevin said to me.

'We'll find out when we have the draw this afternoon and announce the winners.'

'People have written their contact details on the tickets so if they're not in the tearoom for the draw we can still contact them.'

So again, everything was fine and I was enjoying showing customers the new tea shop and soon it was lunchtime. The tearoom was fairly busy.

Elspeth was taking a break and chatting to Janetta and the sewing ladies when Kevin made an announcement.

'Look,' Kevin shouted to Elspeth and the ladies. 'Doyle doesn't have his uniform on.'

I could tell from Elspeth's reaction that she thought Doyle wasn't wearing anything. She dropped her sugar bun and it did cartwheels across the tearoom floor.

There was a similar reaction from other customers and ripples of lustful surprise and anticipation as the women looked round hoping to see Doyle in his birthday suit.

When Elspeth saw the man standing in the tearoom I think her first reaction was — where's Doyle? Then she saw the face smiling anxiously at her. Her eyes widened and her expression was one of sheer glee. She definitely fancied Doyle.

I retrieved the sugar bun and a stray macaron from the floor. Doyle had made an impact on the ladies. They were impressed with him.

'I told you I should interfere,' Kevin said to me.

I smiled at him. 'Do you think he'll ask her out now?'

Kevin nudged me. 'I think he just did. She's nodding.'

Doyle sat down at the table for coffee with Elspeth and the ladies. I'm sure it hadn't been his intention but he was cajoled and pulled into one of the vacant seats by the ladies. Not that he put up a struggle. I think he looked relieved that his casual appearance had gone down well.

Elspeth ran over to me. 'Is it okay if I have another tea with Doyle before I go back behind the front counter?'

'Yes, and give him a slice of Battenberg with his coffee. That's his favourite.'

Doyle caught my attention as I served customers at the next table. We spoke quietly. 'What's the gnome doing back here?'

'Kevin thought he'd found one to match the old one but it's the same gnome. I've told him the truth but Elspeth is none the wiser.'

Doyle laughed.

'Don't laugh. We're raffling him off this afternoon.'

'Kevin or the gnome?'

I smirked. 'Take a guess.'

Doyle held up his ticket. 'If this is the winning ticket I'm melting him down myself.'

Janetta beckoned me over and brought two large garden umbrellas out from under one of the sewing tables. 'You've been so busy I haven't had a chance to give you these. I thought they'd be useful for the garden. They've been in my shed for a couple of years. I never use them.' She gave them to me.

'They look like new.' They were a lovely bright turquoise.

'I've only used them once because they got in the way of my washing line. I'd give them a shake. As I say, they've been in my shed for ages. They've probably got a few spiders inside them.'

I glared at the umbrellas in my hands. 'Kevin,' I yelled and dashed outside to the shed where he was serving tea and slices of cake in the tea shop.

He came hurrying out and I gave him the umbrellas. 'Elspeth's aunt thought we could use these for the garden but I think there are spiders in them. Can you give them a shake over there?' I pointed to an area of the garden away from the shed and the patio.

He laughed. 'You're not bothered by a few wee creepy–crawlies are you, Hazel?'

The speed of my exit answered that question. He was on his own. Although I'd weeded the garden I'd worn gloves and with it being spring I hadn't seen many creepy–crawlies.

'What's Kevin doing with those umbrellas?' a customer asked me.

'He's eh...airing them,' I said. It was true. Sort of.

Doyle had gone and Elspeth confided to me as we worked at the front counter, 'Doyle's asked me to go for a meal with him tonight. I'll have to get my hair done. Can I get away half an hour early?'

'Of course. Leave when you need to. And good luck with your date.'

'Doyle's gorgeous isn't he?' she said. 'I thought he looked sexy in his uniform but he's totally luscious in his ordinary clothes.'

We were chatting about her dinner date when we heard customers laughing and heard screams and chaos coming from the garden.

'I think Kevin's having trouble with the wee spiders,' Janetta said as I hurried to see what was going on.

Kevin was wrestling one of the umbrellas or perhaps he was trying to unravel it. One of the spokes had snagged on his jumper and the spiders had flitted from the umbrella to Kevin.

I laughed. 'You're not bothered by a few wee creepy–crawlies are you, Kevin?'

'Wee creepy–crawlies?' he shouted at me. 'These spiders have got tackety boots on. They're huge.'

So it was Aunt Janetta to the rescue. She unhooked the umbrella spoke from Kevin and shook the spiders on to the grass. She also flicked a few of them off of Kevin's jumper.

The customers were well entertained.

And then it was time for the raffle.

I put the tickets into a cake tin and mixed them around. Then I asked customers in the tearoom to pick out a ticket and hand them to me. I read out the winning numbers. Five customers won a cake each and a few cakes were put aside for those who had won but weren't present. Finally there was the draw for the gnome.

'Would you like to do the honours?' I said to Kevin.

He picked out the winning ticket and read the number aloud.

Elspeth squealed with delight and jumped up holding her ticket. 'I've won.' The customers clapped and cheered.

'The gnome will look lovely in your garden, Elspeth,' I said to her.

'I don't have a garden. I live in a flat, Hazel. But maybe I could keep him outside the shed in the tea shop garden.'

'No,' I protested. And then I smiled. 'No, you should take him home with you. You could put him in your living room or...whatever.'

She considered this for a moment. 'Do people have garden gnomes in their living room?'

No one knew.

'I suppose he'd look sweet beside the fireplace. Yes,' said Elspeth, 'and he'd match my sofa.'

Kevin glanced again at me.

She had a sofa that matched a garden gnome?

Elspeth took the gnome with her when she left early to get her hair done for her hot date with Doyle. The gnome had finally found a home.

'Fancy a cup of tea?' Kevin said as we finished clearing up after everyone had left.

'Thanks.'

He made a pot of tea for two and set our cups on the kitchen table.

'What a day,' I said, sighing.

'The tea shop was popular. We sold a load of cakes and ice cream.'

'I love the shed.'

'Me too,' he said.

We drank our tea and had a natter.

'So what's happening with you and August?'

I told him about the email from Tavish and that he'd been to chat to me in the tearoom.

'Has August contacted you about the message you left for him?'

'No, I thought he'd phone, even to tell me he was mad at me for discussing him with Tavish, but I haven't heard from him all day.'

'What are you going to do?'

'I'm not chasing him. Maybe I won't hear from him again. If he's messing around with Charliss then I'm better off without him.'

'I'm sorry, Hazel.'

I smiled and drank my tea.

'You're going to be late for the pub,' I reminded him.

He downed his tea, grabbed his jacket and waved as he dashed out.

The silence in the tearoom hit me after he'd left. There I was, on my own again. I washed the teacups and started to make dinner for myself. A proper dinner with plenty of vegetables and steak pie.

I was finishing my food when the doorbell rang. August had arrived.

'Have you had dinner?' he said.

'Yes.'

'I was going to invite you over for dinner at my house, but would you like to come over for tea and a chat?' His stunning turquoise eyes looked tired. 'I got your message.'

'And...?'

'And I'd like to talk to you about what Tavish said, what he's accused me of which is basically being a two–timing rat.'

I went with August to his house. He lived in a mansion surrounded by a large garden with lots of trees.

'I'll give you a tour of the beehives later,' he said pointing towards the garden.

We went into his house. It was elegant but not homely. The rich wood flooring and subdued colours were lifted by the glow of the lamps in the main lounge.

A nod to his love of beekeeping was shown in a couple of framed pictures. One looked fairly recent and showed August dressed in an all–in–one white beekeeping suit and a protective hat with a veil. He was wearing gloves and handling a frame of honeycomb buzzing with bees from a hive. The other I guessed was August as a boy standing proudly beside a hive in a wildflower garden with his grandfather.

'Make yourself comfortable,' he said. 'I'll make the tea.'

I heard him rattling around in the kitchen and then he brought the tea through and put it down on the coffee table. We'd hardly said a word in the car. The atmosphere between us was tense.

He'd put biscuits on a plate but neither of us touched them.

He sighed and leaned back in his chair while I sat on the sofa.

'Tavish is trying to cause a rift between us,' he said.

'Why?'

'Because he thinks that I broke up his relationship.'

'He said he was engaged and that you stole her away from him.'

August shook his head. 'I didn't. Even if I had liked her, which I didn't except as a friend, I wouldn't have done that.'

'Why did she leave him?'

'Because she realised that she didn't love him enough. She had started to have feelings for me. But I never encouraged her. I sometimes have business dealings with Tavish over property matters and we attend events and dinners. That's where I met her, a few times, and she got to like me.'

'He said that you dated her before she went away.'

'I didn't. She kept coming round to my house. People thought because she was seen at my house that we were involved. It wasn't true. I think deep down Tavish knows this but he wants to believe it's true so that he can be angry with me. Now he's determined to dish out some payback by making you think that I'm like your ex–boyfriend — a two–timer.'

'So it's not true?'

'No, but I haven't been able to sleep for thinking how to prove this to you. I didn't phone because I didn't know what to say and initially I was so angry that you'd let him come to the tearoom.'

'I shouldn't have done that but I tried to phone you and got no reply.'

'I had to cancel the lecture due to a situation with some of the hives. I left my phone in the house. I didn't get your message until I'd finished.'

I gazed deep into those blue eyes of his. My instincts told me that he was telling the truth. 'You were going to give me a tour of the beehives.'

The tension in him relaxed and he got up from his chair to show me around the property.

I put my coat on and we went outside. Lights illuminated parts of the garden where he kept his hives. The structures were similar to the old hive, made of wood, like little houses. He sounded proud to explain about the garden. 'This area here is sparse this time of year but in the late spring and throughout the summer it's filled with flowers that the bees love.'

I liked the way the garden meandered around the house. He'd created little niches and there were plenty of trees and shrubbery that I pictured would be lovely during the summer. He had a chamomile lawn, a waterfall pond lit up with solar lights and silver birch trees draped with tiny outdoor lights. Paving stones led to different parts of the garden and yet they all led back to the beehives in pride of place in August's garden. Now I realised why his house didn't feel homely. August's world was outside in his garden. It had a magical quality to it.

'I'm out here most nights for hours and during the day. Often I get lost for the time.'

'You obviously love what you do.'

'I love my bees. They're fascinating, enchanting...my grandfather instilled in me an interest in them when I was a boy and that feeling has never waned.'

'There's nothing better than working at something you enjoy.'

He agreed. 'We're both fortunate in that respect.'

I nodded. 'I love to bake.'

By the glow of the garden lights, August pulled me close. 'I'm sorry for all the upset that Tavish caused. I should've dealt with things better but I hope that we can put that behind us.'

I smiled up at him. His blond hair shone under the lights and I'd never seen him look so handsome. My heart ached when I looked at him.

And then he kissed me and all felt right with the world. Despite everything, there was something so right about us, about August. I never thought I'd get involved with a man like him and yet...there I was with the beemaster. Nothing else mattered that evening except our time in the garden.

He eventually drove me home and saw me safely inside the tearoom. We kissed goodnight and then he drove back to his house. We'd agreed to take things at an easy pace. I wondered if everything had gone as smoothly for Elspeth and Doyle.

Kevin had gossip to tell me about Elspeth's dinner date with Doyle the next morning while we put the day's baking in the ovens.

78

'Doyle stopped by the bar on his way home after his date with Elspeth,' said Kevin as he swirled buttercream on to the fairy cakes.

'Did he tell you how it went?'

Kevin tried not to laugh. 'Don't tell Elspeth, but Doyle said that after they'd had a meal in the restaurant they drove back to her flat. They ended up on the sofa in the living room. He said that they were snogging but he couldn't relax because he felt that the gnome was staring at him. It freaked him out and put him off his stride if you know what I mean.'

I nodded. 'Are they going to continue seeing each other?'

'Yes. Doyle made the excuse that he didn't want to take advantage of her on their first date. But it was really your gnome's fault that he didn't stay the night at her flat.'

'What's he going to do about the gnome? Or is he going to take her to his house?'

'A bit of both. They're going to his house tonight, but he's also asked her if she'll give the gnome to a fete event that he's involved in.'

'Doyle's organising a fete?'

Kevin glared at me. 'No, silly. He's just saying that so he can get rid of the gnome. He took the gnome with him. He had it in the boot of the car instead of strapped into the passenger seat.'

We were still talking about this when Elspeth arrived all bright and breezy. Yes, the date had clearly been a success.

'Your hair looks lovely,' I said. It really did.

She fluffed it. 'I'm surprised it's still got some bounce in it.'

Kevin lifted a batch of scones and cakes from the ovens.

While he was busy, Elspeth confided, 'Doyle had his hands all through my hair — and other places.' She giggled and blushed.

'I think you'll make a great couple.'

'So do I,' she said, grinning. 'Doyle was such a gentleman. Even after his hands were everywhere and he had me pinned to the sofa, he restrained himself and left before we went too far. I'd have totally let him so it's just as well that he's the gentlemanly type.'

I saw Kevin's shoulders moving as he overheard what Elspeth said. He was trying not to laugh.

'Is Kevin okay?' she asked me.

'Yes, he eh...got a puff of self–raising flour up his nose.'

She screwed up her face. 'I hate it when that happens. With me, it's icing sugar. That stuff gets everywhere.'

Kevin guffawed.

'I'll make you a cup of tea, Kevin. That'll clear your nostrils for you.'

And off she went to make his tea.

CHAPTER TEN

Trouble at the Tearoom

The next few weeks of spring were a blur of activity. I'd started dating August on a regular basis though he was still a busy man. However, his schedule fitted fine with my work at the tearoom. By April the garden was looking lovely and the tea shop felt as if it had always belonged there. Customers enjoyed having morning and afternoon tea in the shed and by May I was able to keep the tearoom's patio doors open, unless it was a rainy day, allowing customers to wander out into the garden or try a cuppa and cake in the tea shop.

I'd created a vegetable patch behind the shed and had planted lettuce, spring onions, salad carrots and herbs that I picked myself and used for my cooking. Various flowers added fragrance and a pretty niche for customers to unwind. Aunt Janetta's umbrellas were put to use and I'd draped more fairy lights across the branches of the trees.

In the early mornings, when there was dew on the grass, I stood in the garden before starting my baking and breathed in the fresh air. In the heart of the city the garden had a magical and romantic atmosphere. My shed in the city had a welcoming feeling. Even on rainy days customers scurried under umbrellas to snuggle inside and have tea while watching the rain batter off the windows. There was something cosy about it, as if the shed was a hidden gem amid the modern world, a haven of traditional quaintness and relaxation in the fast–paced city.

I earned enough profit from the tearoom and the tea shop to afford the payments on the lease.

Sometimes I slept upstairs in my flat and other times I stayed over at August's house. Bert's shed looked great in August's garden and the second shed was out in the wilds where the other beehives were situated. But I loved the shed at August's mansion, and the hives Bert had built for him were dotted around garden and lit by solar lights in the evenings. It was perfect for romance. But one evening in May something took the shine of its perfection — a gift for August from Bert.

Bert stopped by in his van and was delighted to give August a present, something he'd found near a dump. Bert thought the vintage quality of it would suit August's shed. Oh yes, the gnome was home, sitting beside the shed.

We decided to keep the gnome, at least for a while.

'Maybe he'll disappear,' I said. 'He's a determined wee thing but he never seems to stay anywhere for long.'

August wrapped his arms around me, squeezing me tight. 'Do you ever miss him?'

'The gnome?'

'Your ex–boyfriend.'

'I don't really think of him, except when I see the gnome.'

The night had a warm breeze and we wandered over to sit on one of the benches sheltered by the trees. August put his arm around my shoulders and for a while we sat quite content admiring the garden, the twinkling lights, the scents of the flowers and enjoying the company of each other.

'Charliss handed in her notice,' he said. 'She's leaving Glasgow to work up north in Inverness.'

I restrained myself and did not jump up and down when I heard that news. I trusted August but I'd never trusted Charliss. I felt she often made a play for him and flirted with him every chance she got. He never took her up on her offers of extra activities outside of work, but I was pleased that she'd finally left. I smiled and nodded, but inside I was dancing and celebrating.

'We've been invited to a dinner dance next week at the end of May,' he said. 'It's one of the main events of the year, but Tavish will be there.'

'We should go.'

'There could be trouble.'

'There always is.'

He leaned close and kissed me softly. 'There is when you're involved.'

'Just don't go punching Tavish or slapping him across the jaw.'

'I'll leave that to you, shall I?'

I laughed. 'I promise not to fight with him.'

'Speaking of fighting...you were going to tell me about Kevin punching a customer today at the tearoom.'

'There was a misunderstanding. Kevin was outside in the shed serving cream teas when a man came in and picked on him. He accused Kevin of chatting up his girlfriend at the bar. But the man had him mixed up with someone else. Kevin tried to explain but the man took a wild swing at him so Kevin floored him with a cake stand. Luckily a couple of the police were in having their afternoon scones in the tearoom and they dealt with the man. No harm done. Everything's fine. All we lost was a cream meringue, two rhubarb tarts and a flaky pastry.'

He laughed and we snuggled together on the bench. I felt myself unwind from the hectic day.

'How's the romance between Doyle and Elspeth?' he said.

'They're going on holiday. Doyle's booked a week in Italy for them at the beginning of June. You can imagine how excited Elspeth is. She's never been to Italy.'

'First week in June? I suppose you'll be extra busy with it being just you and Kevin working in the tearoom.'

'Elspeth's Aunt Janetta is coming in to help while Elspeth's on holiday. But...there's a chance that Doyle is going to propose to Elspeth.'

'A proposal huh?'

'Yes, but don't breathe a word of this. Doyle was asking Kevin's advice about buying an engagement ring.'

'Do you think she'll accept if Doyle proposes?'

'With bells on. They're smitten with each other. I wouldn't be surprised if they're married by Christmas.'

'Some people just know when they've met the person they want to spend the rest of their lives with.'

I nodded. 'Elspeth and Doyle are a great couple. If they come back from holiday engaged we'll have a party for them at the tearoom one evening.'

August smiled and then his expression became serious. 'There was something I wanted to talk to you about.'

Before he could tell me I heard a noise. 'Did you hear that?'

August got up from the bench. 'It's the doorbell. Someone's at the front of the house.' He cut through the kitchen, into the hall and opened the door. I followed him. It was around seven in the evening.

Two people wearing identity badges were collecting for a summer charity event. From their conversation, they were used to August giving them items to help out.

'I put these aside for you.' August picked up two large bags filled with...I don't know what...but they seemed very pleased and thanked him.

'The gardening items you gave us last year sold well,' one of them said. 'Thanks again for helping us.'

August glanced round at me as if suddenly remembering something. 'I think there's something else that you could take with you,' he said to them while staring at me.

He hurried out to the garden and came back carrying the gnome.

I nodded, and he handed him over.

We finally waved goodbye to the gnome.

We stood in the doorway and watched them drive off.

'He'll be back,' I said. 'Will we have a bet? I give it five or six weeks.'

'I'll see you on that and raise you to ten weeks though I could be a little optimistic.' He sighed deeply. 'At least now I'll be able to ask you something without having him, a shadow of the past, in our lives.'

I smiled up at him. 'Ask me what? Not to wear a sequin dress to the dinner dance? Not to wrestle with Tavish? Not to go near the beehives without the proper clothing?'

'Now that's one thing I've repeatedly warned you about.'

'I didn't touch the hives. I was only peeking in at the bees.'

He shook his head, grinned and pulled me close. 'Whatever am I going to do with you, Hazel?'

He kissed me and I forgot about everything. In that moment there was just us. I was happy with August, happier and more content than I'd ever been in my entire life. So in a way I had the tearoom to thank for that. I remembered the day August walked in to buy the beehive cake. He looked so handsome — all blond hair, rugged looks and eyes the colour of a turquoise sea.

But some moments don't last...

August led me by the hand back out to the garden. We stood under the bough of the old lavender trees that arched across part of the lawn near the pond. The air was warm and clear.

I had a sense of dread as he stood in front of me. He looked anxious.

'What's wrong? What is it you want to ask me?'

'I wondered...I thought...would you marry me, Hazel?'

Marry him?

The words startled me and then I gave him my answer.

'Yes, I'd love to marry you.' I threw my arms around him and held him tight.

He glanced up at one of the trees. My eyes widened. I hadn't even noticed when I'd walked past earlier. A diamond ring was hanging from one of the branches. The diamonds sparkled in the twilight.

August reached up for the ring and then put it on my finger. Diamonds set in gold scintillated in the light.

'If you don't like it...I can exchange it for another ring. But I think this would be a perfect match with a wedding band of gold, don't you?'

I nodded. 'A perfect match.' Just like August and me.

I may have put more lights on the trees and the tea shop shed than necessary. The tearoom garden glowed like a beacon in the night.

We'd invited around fifty guests to celebrate our engagement. Kevin baked us a cake in the shape of a shed and added fondant flowers and bumblebees.

'I'd like to propose a toast,' said Kevin, 'to the happy couple on their engagement.'

He glanced at Doyle who gave him a wink. The gossip confirmed that Doyle was indeed going to propose to Elspeth when they went on holiday.

Everyone raised their glasses and tea cups and drank a toast to us that evening.

We were overwhelmed with gifts. Kevin gave us a vintage cake stand. Elspeth, Janetta and the sewing women had made us a gorgeous quilt for our bed. They'd sewn cake designs and bumblebees into the pattern.

Everyone was so kind and thoughtful and the party was going well until Bert and Bridie arrived and presented us with a gift each. Bert had made a beehive for August in the style of a wedding cake.

It was a bit of a novelty but beautifully handcrafted and August was really pleased with it.

Then Bert stepped forward and gave me a large gift bag with something he thought I'd love inside it.

'It's a perfect match,' said Bert.

I opened the bag, which was quite heavy, and there gazing at me with his beady eyes and corrugated iron hair was the gnome.

'He's just like the one I gave to August. Now you're a couple with a couple of gnomes.' Bert and Bridie smiled at me so I put the gnome over beside the shed and thanked them for their gift.

'Can I fill up your champagne glass?' Kevin whispered to me.

'Yes, to the brim.'

Janetta was a great help in the tearoom when Elspeth was away on holiday. Doyle proposed to her the first evening they arrived in Italy and we'd had several excited phone calls from Elspeth squealing with delight. He'd presented her with a vintage diamond and ruby engagement ring that she went cock–a–hoop over. I think it was a wise decision on Doyle's part to propose early in the holiday so that Elspeth had a week to calm down.

When she came back we had an engagement party for her and this time I baked a cake for them — a traditional cake with royal icing and fondant tea roses.

The shed in the city had now hosted two engagement parties since its opening and this gave me the idea that I'd make the tearoom garden and tea shop shed available to hire for private parties such as birthdays and engagements.

By mid–June I had a few bookings.

After a hectic day at the tearoom when everyone had gone home, I opened the patio doors and let the warm night air waft in from the garden. It was a Tuesday evening, and I was looking forward to a quiet night sewing and pottering around in the garden. August was working so I had the entire night to myself.

The evening was a scorcher. I sewed part of a wrap around skirt that I was making for myself, but then the hot night tempted me outside to the garden. I put two scoops of vanilla ice cream into a tall glass of iced lemonade and sat on a chair outside the shed admiring the flowers and unwinding.

The previous night I'd been in a crafty mood and had painted various bits and pieces in the tea shop and tearoom lovely pinks, pale blues and soft lemon shades. I'd bought a set of new paints and had gone a bit wild mixing the colours and painting anything that I thought needed a whole new look.

As I sat in the garden enjoying my ice cream drink, I looked at the gnome. His beady eyes and sour expression needed cheering up. I finished my drink and then set up my paints. Starting with his face, I painted over his disapproving expression and then gave him a smile and bright–eyed look.

'There,' I said to him. 'That's better.'

I gave the rest of him a fresh coat of paint as well. By the time I'd finished with him he looked like a whole new gnome. He still had the dent in his bum but well...you can't have everything.

I hung him up to dry by his arse handle so that everything from his clothes to the bobble on his hat would dry without sticking to the grass or flowers. He dangled high above the entrance to the patio doors on a rail that was part of a canopy. I reckoned he'd be dry within the hour.

Realising I'd somehow managed to get paint on my shoes and my clothes, I opened the side gates rather than trail a mess through the centre of the tearoom floor. As I was only going to be a few minutes to clean myself up, I left the side gates unlocked while I kicked my shoes off at the front door of the tearoom and ran upstairs to the flat. I'd even got paint on my socks. That gnome was nothing but trouble.

When I came back down I saw Tavish's sports car parked outside the tearoom. I looked up and down the street. There was no sign of him. I secured the premises, locked the side gates and as I headed into the tearoom kitchen I saw Tavish outside in the garden.

Damn him! I'd only left the side entrance open for five minutes and that prat had used it to get into the garden.

I stormed out of the tearoom and shouted at him. 'What the blazes are you doing here? And how dare you come in without being invited.'

He didn't flinch. Dressed in his suit he wandered over to the shed. 'Very quaint. Very nice, Hazel. You've got everything looking lovely.' He sat down on my chair and relaxed.

'Don't bother getting comfy,' I snapped at him. 'You're not welcome here.'

'I came to apologise,' he began. 'I've already apologised to August and although I know we'll never be friends, we've agreed to draw a line under the past, any difference we've had, any squabbles and fights, and try to get along a bit better.'

I blinked. 'What's the catch?' He had to have a motive.

'I heard about your engagement. Congratulations by the way. I can see from here that the ring's a dazzler. Not quite as spectacular as that sparkly red dress of yours, but anyway...I'd like us not be adversaries any more.'

'And has August agreed to wipe the slate clean?'

'He has. So now it's up to you, Hazel. It's become awkward when we're meeting at dinners and events, and I'm trying to be less of a troublemaker these days. I'm getting too old for such nonsense.'

'Okay. But you can't waltz into my premises like this ever again.'

'Sorry...sorry...'

He seemed to be trying to make things friendly so I offered him an iced drink or a coffee before he left.

'Whatever you're having.'

'I was about to have another ice cream and lemonade drink.'

His face brightened. 'I haven't had one of those in years.'

I went into the tearoom kitchen and scooped ice cream into two tall glasses and topped them up with lemonade. I served them with a long silver spoon in each glass.

I was about to carry them through the tearoom when I heard a thud, a yell and another thud followed by mumbling and moaning.

I put the drinks down and ran through to see what had happened.

Tavish was lying on the patio slightly stunned from being hit on the head by the garden gnome. I guessed that I hadn't tied him up securely or...perhaps it was just one of those things. It wasn't my fault that the gnome had whacked him on the head. I pictured the gossip — rich prat nobbled by garden gnome.

I tried not to laugh as Tavish rubbed his head and staggered to his feet, glaring daggers at the gnome. He went to boot the gnome across the garden but I stopped him.

'Don't kick my gnome,' I warned him. I lifted the gnome and put him beside the shed. The little smile on his face made me smile too.

'I'm glad you find it funny, Hazel.'

'It's a handy thing that we're friends now, isn't it?'

Tavish swallowed his anger and forced a smile.

Then he left.

I stirred my ice cream drink and relaxed in the garden.

August phoned me. 'Tavish called me to complain about being hit by a garden ornament. A gnome.'

I explained what had happened. I also told him that I'd repainted the gnome and given him a smile.

'You know, Hazel, there are times when I wish you weren't a magnet for trouble and other times when I love you for it — especially when Tavish is on the receiving end of it.'

'How are things tonight with the bees?' I asked him.

'Busy. How is everything at the shed in the city?'

I breathed in the warm summer air and admired the garden. The gnome with his new happy expression sat contended nearby. 'Everything's great. See you in the morning?'

'Yes. I love you, Hazel.'

He went to hang up.

'But there's just one thing that you should know,' I told him.

'What's that?' he said.

'I'm keeping the gnome.'

I heard August laugh. 'See you in the morning, darling.'

I sipped my ice cream lemonade beside my shed in the city.

The lights of Glasgow sparkled all around the garden against the clear summer night sky.

And all was right with the world.

End

About the Author:

Follow De-ann on Instagram @deann.black

De-ann Black is a bestselling author, scriptwriter and former newspaper journalist. She has over 70 books published. Romance, crime thrillers, espionage novels, action adventure. And children's books (non-fiction rocket science books and children's fiction). She became an Amazon All-Star author in 2014 and 2015.

She previously worked as a full-time newspaper journalist for several years. She had her own weekly columns in the press. This included being a motoring correspondent where she got to test drive cars every week for the press for three years.

Before being asked to work for the press, De-ann worked in magazine editorial writing everything from fashion features to social news. She was the marketing editor of a glossy magazine. She is also a professional artist and illustrator. Fabric design, dressmaking, sewing, knitting and fashion are part of her work.

Additionally, De-ann has always been interested in fitness, and was a fitness and bodybuilding champion, 100 metre runner and mountaineer. As a former N.A.B.B.A. Miss Scotland, she had a weekly fitness show on the radio that ran for over three years.

De-ann trained in Shukokai karate, boxing, kickboxing, Dayan Qigong and Jiu Jitsu. She is currently based in Scotland.

Her colouring books and embroidery design books are available in paperback. These include Floral Nature Embroidery Designs and Scottish Garden Embroidery Designs.

Find out more at: www.de-annblack.com

Printed in Great Britain
by Amazon

21060293R00054